Heart Story

A Metamorphic Odyssey

into the

Heart of Human Consciousness

10th Anniversary Revised Edition 2024

Gabriel Iqbal

Heart Story
A Metamorphic Odyssey into the Heart of Human Consciousness
Copyright © 2014 by Gabriel Iqbal
10th Anniversary Revised Edition 2024
All rights reserved
ASIN: B00P86M0BS
ISBN-13: 978-1503361119
ISBN-10: 150336111X

This book or any portion thereof may not be reproduced or used in any manner whatsoever without the express written permission of the publisher except for the use of brief quotations in a book review.

Cover picture: The cover features a profound artistic rendering of Omar Khayyam—revered polymath, poet, astronomer, and mathematician—portrayed in the intricate and symbolically rich aesthetic of Safavid-era Persian miniature art. This visual composition transcends mere portraiture, serving as a metaphysical tableau that evokes elevated states of spiritual consciousness. Ethereal figures, depicted as celestial or spirit beings, are shown ceremonially pouring wine—an enduring Sufi metaphor for the elixir of divine ecstasy and the awakening of the heart to transcendental truths. This symbolic liberation does not signify hedonism but rather the dissolution of ego-bound intellect into a state of mystical union. Adjacent to this, a delicately rendered harp subtly echoes the haunting resonance of divine separation, signifying the soul's yearning pangs for reunion with the Beloved—a core theme in Persian mystic poetry. The entire imagery thus becomes a visual exegesis of Khayyam's philosophical and poetic legacy, interweaving cosmology, metaphysics, and the aesthetics of love.

Category: Visionary Metaphysics - Poetry

Published under license by Eureka Academy - Canada
Tel: +1 647-782-1115   Fax: +1 905-257-8077
email: eurekaacademycanada@gmail.com
www.eurekamakingadifference.com

Also see the masterpiece work by the author on:
www.heartintelligencebook.com

Shams and Rumi
Transcendental Journey

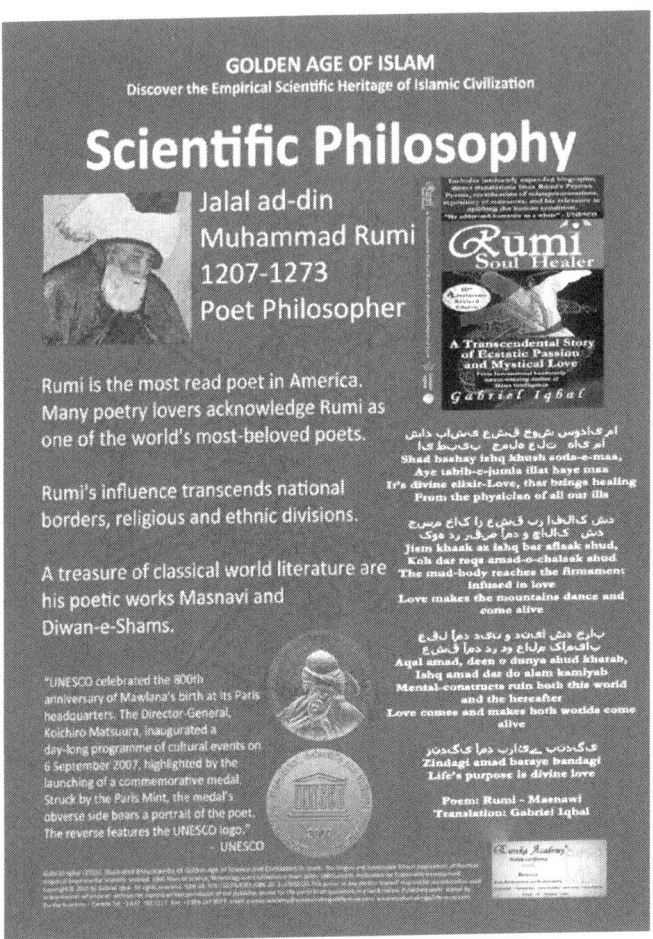

Iqbal, Gabriel (2025). *Illustrated Encyclopedia of Golden Age of Science and Civilization in Islam.* Eureka Academy, Canada

HEART STORY

"Inside my heart there is
A temple, a synagogue, a church, a mosque,
A monastery, a fish market
A serene lake, a tempestuous sea
Agreements and disagreements
Glory and failure
A big bang at dawn and a little bang at dusk
All the cries, aspirations and silent prayers
Yearning and seeking
Everything disintegrates and dissolves
In a tempestuous ocean
Finally unifies
Collapses on one altar
In one Breath
In God"

Gabriel Iqbal

Contents

10th Anniversary Revised Edition ....

Acknowledgements ....

International Acclaim for the Author 1

About the Author 6

Preview 9

Introduction 13

Chapter 1: The Blundering Fanatic 26

God, Let's Talk 38

Chapter 2: The Accident – An Existential Collision 50

Chapter 3: Mystical Journey with Lalla – The Dervish-Woman 56

Salsabīl 56
   Qur'anic and Philosophical Context: 57
   Spiritual and Symbolic Implications: 58

Inner Visions and the Parables of Lalla 64
   The Parable of the Mirror 65
   The Parable of the Forgotten Seed 66
   The Parable of the Burning Book 68

Transformative Wisdom through Mystical Allegory 69
   Sufi Parable of the Pond Fish 69
   The Merchant and the Parrot: The Allegory of

Transcendence 71
The Farmer's Son: The Reciprocity of Virtue 73
The Paradox of Ungratefulness 75
The Hermit and the Fish: The Folly of Ignorant Compassion 76
Carrying Your Troubles: The Alchemy of Catharsis 78
The Parable of the Movie Star... 80
The Parable of the Tortoise and the Hare 81
The Buddha's Refusal to Name the Divine..................... 82
Abraham and the Iconoclasm of Thought: A Metaphysical Parable... 94
Mystical Exposition: Rūmī's Iconoclasm Beyond Stone and Concept 95
The Real Idol: Religious Ego and Institutional Power 98
The Native American Parable: "The Wolf I Nourish" .. 106
Gabriel's Parable of Creative Design: A Dialectic on Rationality and Transcendence 108
Gabriel's Parable of Avoiding Imitation: The Peril of Mimicry 109
Gabriel's Parable of the Two Brothers and Their Sister: Paths of Knowing 110
Gabriel's Parable of the Paradox of Truth 111
Gabriel's Parable of the Controlling Mother: The Intergenerational Cycle 112
Gabriel's Parable of Woman is Creative, Man is Created 112
Gabriel's Parable of Celebrating the Flight of Our Little Bird 114
Gabriel's Parable of Do Not Live by Other People's Opinions of You.. 115

Odes of Solomon *118*

Chapter 4: Mystical Journey with Lao Tzu – The Inter-

Galactic Sage 120

    The River That Remembers 123
    The Bird That Would Not Fly 124
    The Mirror That Refused to Break 125
    The Path That Walks Itself 128
    Epilogue: The Inner Shrine 129
    Zen Koan of the Bamboo: The Parable of Delayed Bloom 130
    Zen Koan of the Old Man's Horse: The Dialectic of Fortune and Misfortune 131
    Zen Koan of the Sound of One Hand Clapping: The Practice of Wu Wei 133
    Zen Koan of the Two Hermits: Letting Go of Dogma 134
    Zen Koan of Finding Wisdom: The Ordeal of Readiness 136
    Zen Koan of the Teacup: Emptiness as Prerequisite for Learning 137
    Zen Koan of Finding a Piece of the Truth: The Perils of Premature Certainty 138
    Zen Koan of Is That So: The Power of Equanimity 140
    Zen Koan of Right and Wrong: Compassion Beyond Judgment 141
    Zen Koan of Nothing Exists: The Limits of Nihilistic Cognition 141
    Zen Koan of The Light: Bearing the Lantern 142
    Zen Koan of I Don't Know Who I Am But I Am Awake: The Paradox of Identity 143
    Zen Koan of The Other Side: Relativity of Perspective 144
    Zen Koan of Doing One Thing at a Time: The Essence of Focus 145
    Zen Koan of Knowing When Enough Is Enough: The Wisdom of Sufficiency 146

Chapter 5: Mystical Journey with Nasrudin – The Witty

Metaphysical Doctor 148

    Nasrudin's Sufi Parable of the Lost Donkey.................. 149
    Nasrudin's Sufi Parable of the Moon's Supremacy over the
    Sun 150
    Nasrudin's Sufi Parable of 'Seeing in the Dark' 151
    Nasrudin's Sufi Parable of the Father, the Son, and the
    Donkey.. 152
    Nasrudin's Trial Before the King 154

Chapter 6: Transcendental Return via Stairway To Heaven 156

Chapter 7: Wisdom of the Ages from Shams Tabriz........166

Bibliography 171

Publications by the Author 177

    Books and Films.. 177

    Environmental Research Publications 179

    Leadership Development Research Publications 181

Customer Review..183

Heart Intelligence Film Documentary

Available for viewing at no cost as a public education enterprise on:

www.heartintelligencebook.com

HEART STORY

Comprehensive Illustration to Show the Common Principles of Humanity in All Faiths

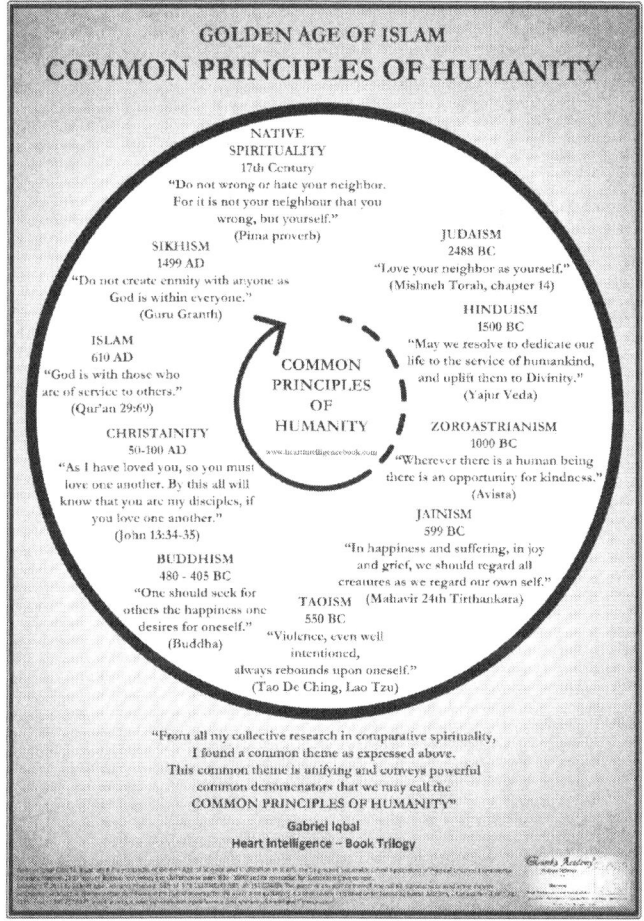

Iqbal, Gabriel (2025). *Illustrated Encyclopedia of Golden Age of Science and Civilization in Islam.* Eureka Academy, Canada
A high resolution digital version of the Common Principles of Humanity is available on www.gabrieliqbal.com

Comprehensive Illustration to Show the Common Concept of God in All Faiths

Iqbal, Gabriel (2025). *Illustrated Encyclopedia of Golden Age of Science and Civilization in Islam.* Eureka Academy, Canada

A high resolution digital version of God – as Experienced in Different Faiths is available on: www.gabrieliqbal.com

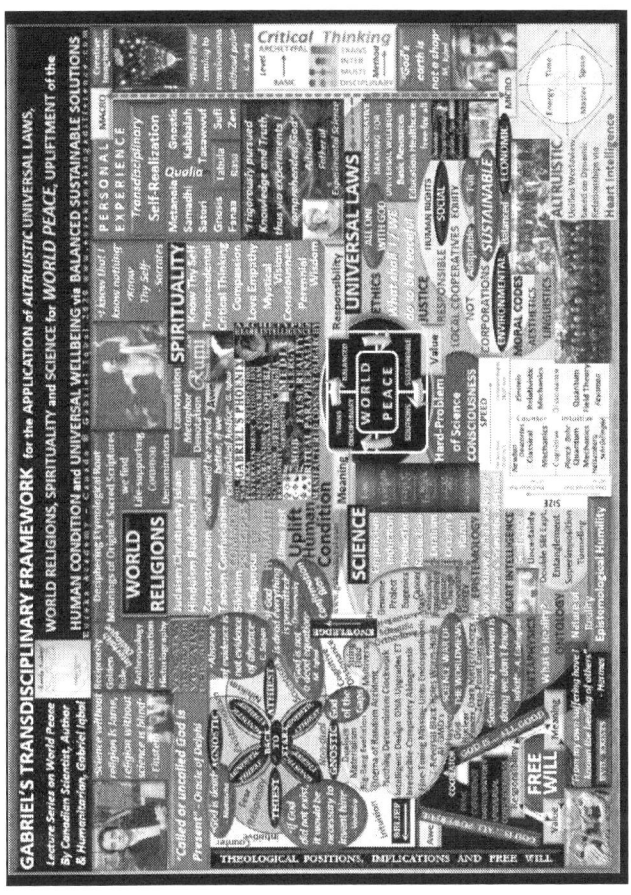

A high resolution digital version of the Framework is available on: www.gabrieliqbal.com

10ᵗʰ Anniversary Revised Edition

It has been 10 years since the first publication of Heart Story in 2014. Major changes and additions have been introduced in this revised 10ᵗʰ Anniversary edition of 2024.

English translation of Rūmī's poems is rendered directly from Persian, meticulously preserving the depth, context, and profound significance of the original verses.

Qur'anic verses are examined through the lens of classical Arabic as preserved in Edward William Lane's Arabic-English Lexicon, one of the most authoritative resources on classical Arabic root meanings, supported with original Qur'anic Arabic, transliteration, translation, and etymological analysis.

English translation of Rūmī's poems is rendered directly from Persian, meticulously preserving the depth, context, and profound significance of the original verses.

Acknowledgements

To my family and friends,
for your love and encouragement.

International Acclaim for the Author

"Gabriel is a truly passionate
and motivating...
You will think about his
work long after it is over."

- Sheridan College, Canada

-

"Gabriel is absolutely correct –
In order to get out of the mess we're in,
we need a paradigm shift,
a different way of seeing ourselves
on the planet."

- Dr. David Suzuki, Science broadcaster and environmental activist, Canada

-

"As a result of Gabriel's extensive experience as an environmental scientist, he has a great deal to offer in today's classroom. His passion, connections and experience in this area will be invaluable in preparing students to steward the world of the future." "Gabriel leads by example and has successfully started the first active recycling program at the school." "Gabriel has an unrelenting passion for teaching science that comes out when you talk to him. Some people are good at what they do- some love what they do – Gabriel has both."

- Chisholm Academy, Canada

-

"Gabriel has bought a lot of fresh lateral thinking and out of the box solutions." "His involvement and enthusiasm is commendable and a breath of fresh air in our organization."

- Kempinski, Switzerland

"Gabriel has uncovered the mechanics
of the flow of creativity within
each of us and between each of
our team members.
Gabriel's genuine follow-ups and
individual consultation with our
team members makes his
contributions both unique and
very appreciable. We recommend
Gabriel's services to all who
seek continued development and
a vision to prosper in a well-balanced culture."

- Novell, USA

-

"Gabriel Makes The Difference."
"Gabriel walks the talk."
"This is a timely message."

- Peel Multicultural Council, Canada

-

"Gabriel is a joy to work with
and as a leader inspires the team
in an unconventional
yet powerful manner.

He played a key role in
the improvement of quality.
Gabriel has always amazed us as
a human being as someone
who comes across
very different from the crowd."

- Tyco International, USA

-

"Gabriel shows an exceptional interest
in biological study and produces
above standard, accurate
and well expressed work."

**- Ealing, Hammersmith and
West London College, UK**

-

"Gabriel is a committed and pragmatic
business professional and brings
about the best of dedicated team
dynamics and planning of
organizational structure within the
administrative systems of his
corporate clients." "Gabriel is
passionate about what he refers
to as Information Age Team

Dynamics that are far advanced then the Industrial Age organizational systems."

- BTL Worldwide, Dubai

-

"Amazing, we have learnt so much."

- George Brown College, Canada

-

About the Author

Gabriel Iqbal is a Canadian award-winning and internationally acclaimed scientist, author, poet and humanitarian. He designs the curriculum, teaches the International Baccalaureate Diploma Program in Biology and Theory of Knowledge, and heads the department of science at his current post.

After having secured a scholarship for distinguished performance in a Diploma in Health Sciences at Ealing, Hammersmith and West London College, UK, in the early 1990's, he was privileged to work under one of the world's eminent Biologist, Dr. Ray McNeil Alexander and earned a BSc. Honours in Biology from the University of Leeds, UK, with a key focus on Human Evolution. Later, he completed a Post-Graduation in Science Education with a specialism in History of Science from the same university and taught science for several years. Further, his career focused on Lean Management,

Sustainable Development, Organisational Behaviour, and Wellbeing. He has worked internationally for almost 30 years and has written multiple books and encyclopedias encompassing transdisciplinary subjects.

Gabriel is also a paradigm-shifting Lean Management Certified Trainer and a Certified Internal Auditor for Environmental Health and Safety Management Systems which includes ISO 14001 (Environmental Management Systems Training) and OHSAS 18001 (Occupational Health and Safety Management Systems Training). Gabriel has provided Ethical Leadership, Management, Corporate and Social Responsibility, Human Motivation, Sustainable Development and Wellbeing Programs via his training and development organisation, the Eureka Academy:

www.eurekamakingadifference.com

Gabriel's major work is represented in, "*Heart Intelligence*" book, which is accompanied by a non-profit Film:

www.heartintelligencebook.com

Gabriel's books and encyclopedias are available on Amazon:

www.amazon.com/Gabriel-Iqbal/e/B00PTJ0OIK

For his international work and services, Gabriel has received the following awards:

- **Making a Difference Award 2011**
  Peel Multicultural Council, Canada

- **Outstanding Guest Speaker Award 2010**
  International Leadership Congress

- **International e-learning Award 2011**
  International e-learning Congress

Gabriel is also a member of the Royal Society of Science, London, UK and the Library of Congress, Washington, US.

Preview

10th Anniversary edition of 2024

Major changes and additions have been introduced in this revised edition.

Transcendental Odyssey

Heart Story unfolds as a profound transcendental odyssey charting the inner transformation of a protagonist named Alpha, who embarks on a deeply personal quest to transcend the confines of suffering and awaken to a higher dimension of being. Along this transcendent journey, Alpha encounters three pivotal archetypes who serve as catalytic agents of his evolution: Lalla, a Dervish-Woman embodying feminine metaphysical wisdom; Lao Tzu, envisioned as an inter-galactic sage who imparts the Tao's cosmic truths; and Nasrudin, the mystical jester whose paradoxical wit unveils hidden realities. As Alpha approaches the culmination of his metamorphosis, the sublime presence of Rūmī enters, guiding him toward the ineffable flowering of what the author terms "Heart Intelligence".

Voyage and Visionary Apparitions

Appearing in the liminal background of Alpha's voyage are visionary apparitions of revered mystics, philosophers, scientists, poets, and spiritual reformers—including Rūmī, Shams Tabrīz, Leo Tolstoy, Carl Jung, Johann Wolfgang von Goethe, Ralph Waldo Emerson, Mark Twain, Ibn Arabi, Jiddu Krishnamurti, Hafiz, Voltaire, Omar Khayyam, Leonardo da Vinci, Khalil Gibran, Mansur Al-Hallaj, Rabia al-Basri, William Blake, Meister Eckhart, Joan of Arc, George Bernard Shaw, Bulleh Shah, Moses Maimonides, Hermes Trismegistus, Muhammad Iqbal, Albert Einstein, and others—who collectively serve as archetypal soul-guides. These luminous figures emerge through dreamlike interludes, functioning as metaphysical signposts that navigate Alpha through parallel dimensions, Zen koans, Sufi allegories, and epiphanic meta-visions that deconstruct the limits of cognitive intelligence and ignite a revelatory explosion the author designates as *Heart Intelligence*—a paradigm of wholistic, compassion-centered awareness.

Emissaries of Peace and Compassion

Throughout the narrative, emissaries of peace and compassion from diverse religious traditions and philosophical lineages make brief, poignant appearances to share the original, unadulterated message of unconditional love, artistic luminosity, and the latent unity underpinning human existence. Their shared invocation invites the reader to discern a universal denominator embedded within the essence of all great spiritual traditions—a sacred call toward global oneness and integrative consciousness. This convergence of archetypal mentors animates a powerfully transformative and passionately charged journey—one imbued with melancholy, wit, allegory, adventure, epistemological humility and the poetic grace of what the author evocatively describes as *Heart-Metamorphosis Through Heart Intelligence for Upliftment of the Human Condition*.

Direct Translations

Gabriel Iqbal is a Canadian scientist, poet, author, and humanitarian who has traveled and lived across the Turko-Persian Central Asian belt and knows the Persian language. In this book Gabriel has directly translated the Rūmī Poems from the original Persian. He is especially noted for his emphasis on the original message of Rūmī for the pragmatic upliftment of the human condition through justice, altruistic behaviour and the universal oneness of mankind.

Psycho-Spiritual Alchemy

Heart Story thus becomes a literary expression of psycho-spiritual alchemy—a work that both complements and expands the author's magnum opus, *Heart Intelligence: Book and Film*. Through it, Gabriel constructs a multidimensional framework of self-realization. *Heart Story* is not merely a narrative; it is an invocation—a gem-like vessel of illumination—designed to awaken the numinous depths of the human spirit and infuse even the darkest interior landscapes with the radiant light of awakened consciousness.

> *"Omar Khayyam, the sage of star and scroll,*
> *In Safavid hues, his tale is whole.*
> *A poet's gaze, an astral mind,*
> *With math and verse, the Truth aligned.*
> *In sacred strokes of Persian art,*
> *He stands—a mirror of the heart.*
> *The wine, by spirit hands outpoured,*
> *Awakens souls to love adored.*
> *No drunken jest, but mystic fire,*
> *A nectar drawn from heart's desire.*
> *The harp resounds with aching grace,*
> *For longing hearts in God's embrace.*
> *Each string, a sigh for realms above,*
> *Each note, the pangs of parting love.*
> *In every line, the veil grows thin—*
> *The cosmos speaks, and dwells within."*

Gabriel Iqbal

Introduction

Mystical traditions often affirm the profound and elegantly simple axiom that there exist as many interpretations of a narrative as there are stars scattered across the cosmos. In this spirit, *Heart Story* is not a static text bound by the confines of a singular, definitive meaning. Rather, it is a living tapestry—an ever-unfolding constellation of interpretive possibilities that invite infinite subjective engagement.

This work resists the imposition of a canonical or authoritative reading. Instead, it beckons the reader to enter into an intimate dialogical relationship with the text. I urge you, therefore, not merely to consume the story passively, seeking prescriptive meanings, but to become a co-creator of its significance. Let the narrative serve as a reflective surface—a mirror in which your own inner landscapes are revealed, refracted, and reimagined.

In surrendering to this dynamic process, you may experience what the mystics describe as a "metamorphosis of the heart"—a transformative awakening whereby the intuitive intelligence embedded within the story's deeper consciousness ignites your own heart's insight. If you allow this unfolding, you may find yourself traversing realms of unbounded perception and insight, where each reading becomes an act of creative transcendence and each interpretation a portal to new existential possibilities.

برخیز و مخور غم جهان، کاری کن
چون شمع در این محفل جان، نوری کن
گر سنگ گران‌باری و گر کوهی سخت
بشکن، بگذر، برو، جهان نوری کن

"Barkhīz o makhor gham-i jahān, kārī kun
Chun shamʿ dar īn mahfil-i jān, nūrī kun
Gar sang-i girānbārī o gar kūhī sakht
Bishkan, bugzar, burō, jahān nūrī kun"

"Rise! Do not sit mourning over the world's grief—**act!**
Be as a flame in this gathering of souls, radiating light.
Even if you are a heavy stone or an immovable mountain,
Break, transcend, advance—***illumine the world!"***

Shams Tabriz

The authentic narrative of humanity is fundamentally the pursuit of self-realization; all other aspects of existence are peripheral—a shell encasing the true core. The essential "seed" of our being is nestled in the heart of the self-actualized individual. *Heart Story* represents an interpretive endeavour to access this deeper truth through the lens of spiritual and mystical traditions. The term "reach" feels inadequate in this context, for the journey is not an external seeking, but rather an inward pilgrimage—a descent into the innermost sanctum of consciousness, often symbolized as the *essence of the heart.*

Within the traditions of Zen Buddhism and Islamic Sufism, *Koans* and *Parables* respectively serve as epistemological instruments intended to dismantle linear cognition. These paradoxical narratives are meditative catalysts, crafted not to inform but to transform. They function as metaphysical riddles that bypass rational thought, evoking a moment of *satori* or sudden illumination through intuitive insight.

My experiential and research engagement with these symbolic forms has led me to interpret them as layered conduits of meaning, including but not limited to:

- A metaphysical *step backward*, which paradoxically reveals a more expansive landscape.
- A conscious *suspension of control*—the willingness to relinquish resistance and allow solutions to emerge from realms beyond limiting comprehensions.
- A surrender of cognitive dominance, enabling a broader and deeper perception—where the *ocean appears vaster, and the sky wider.*

- Moments of piercing clarity (*aha!* experiences) that emerge without theatrical display or dogmatic discursive reasoning.
- Insights that elude linguistic articulation—their essence remaining subtle, nuanced, and ultimately transcendental.
- Evolving interpretations, shaped by the consciousness and readiness of the observer.
- Sudden awareness that love transcends cognition—a *gnosis* that is more felt than explained.
- Nature's intrinsic intelligence made manifest through silence, reflection, and a posture of epistemic humility.
- The imaginative and emotive faculties—*wit and fervor*—required to navigate the inherent unpredictability of existence.
- A transformation of the heart through *Heart Intelligence*, invoking an inner alchemy.
- Love of humanity as a metaphysical solvent, dissolving the density of intellect and revealing wonder, spontaneity, and multidimensional awareness.

In both Zen and Sufi traditions, the Koan or Parable operates as a meditative solution—a layer to be penetrated through contemplation. These are not meant to be intellectually deciphered but rather engaged with as vehicles for inner dissolution. The intent is to fatigue the analytical faculties, producing a "withdrawal" from over-dependence on reason, thus opening the psyche to insights that arise from a heart-centered, intuitive substratum of awareness.

Approximately 1,700 Zen koans and countless Sufi parables have been preserved across diverse spiritual and philosophical traditions. These narratives, rooted in the lived wisdom of ancient Zen and Sufi masters, serve as timeless pedagogical tools designed to provoke introspection, disrupt linear cognition, and illuminate non-dualistic insight. Over the years, I have encountered these profound expressions of spiritual intelligence through reading and oral transmission across various cultural contexts, consistently observing their ability to transcend geographic, religious, and epistemological boundaries.

In *Heart Story*, a curated selection of Zen koans and Sufi parables are not merely presented but reinterpreted through the lens of my own autobiographical reflections and inner experiences. These interpretations aim to reveal the layered and often non-literal dimensions of such teachings, emphasizing their capacity to *activate expanded states of consciousness*. Additionally, I have contributed original narratives inspired by visionary encounters and *altered states*—what may be termed *meta-visions*—aimed at exploring the architecture of transcendental awareness.

Each story is accompanied by an analytical exposition elucidating its implications for cognitive, emotional, and ethical decision-making. The objective is to foster open-ended awareness, stimulate multidimensional problem-solving, and cultivate the cognitive flexibility necessary for navigating the ambiguities and paradoxes inherent in daily life. This work thus aspires to bridge contemplative traditions with pragmatic application, offering a psychospiritual framework for integrative insight and adaptive action.

Throughout the narrative, a series of concise yet profound parables—drawing from Zen, Sufi, and other timeless wisdom traditions—are interwoven into the protagonist Alpha's transformative journey toward reawakening self-awareness. These illustrative stories serve not merely as philosophical interludes but as essential didactic tools, elucidating the paradoxes and contradictions inherent in human existence. Through them, the text explores how individuals can cultivate resilience and equanimity in the face of life's inevitable upheavals, learning to navigate its cyclical challenges with insight, grace, and inner clarity.

The archetypal figures of Lalla, Lao Tzu, and Nasrudin stand among the emissaries of inner peace, mystical insight, and metaphysical wisdom within the global canon of aphoristic literature. Each represents a distinct spiritual tradition—Lalla embodying the soul of Kashmiri mysticism and Sufi devotion, Lao Tzu articulating the foundational principles of Taoist philosophy, and Nasrudin offering profound transcendental truths through paradox and wit. Collectively, they function as enduring custodians of contemplative consciousness, whose teachings transcend cultural boundaries and serve as perennial guides for those seeking harmony, and the dissolution of ego-bound perception.

In the final phase of Alpha's existential journey, the presence of Rūmī emerges as a transcendent force, bringing a profound sense of inner peace and resolution to Alpha's previously restless and fragmented soul. Rūmī's spiritual influence does not merely soothe but catalyzes a deeper self-realization—an ontological reorientation from fragmentation to unity.

Looming silently yet powerfully in the background are the seers, sages, and mystics of human history—figures whose poetic utterances and metaphysical reflections offer transformative insights. Their expressions transcend the confines of binary thought and empirical cognition, dissolving the artificial boundaries that separate self from other, subject from object. Through their wisdom, a deeper epistemic shift is initiated: one that invites meta-cognition, introspective clarity, and a direct experience of non-duality—an awareness often described as the realization of the interconnectedness of all things, or the mystical perception of *"Everything as One."*

A more extensive and integrative exploration of these self-realized beings and their contributions to the evolution of human consciousness is presented in *"Heart Intelligence"* and *"The Book of Wellbeing"*, where their teachings are examined as catalysts for both personal and collective transcendence.

These poems reflect a central Sufi theme in Rūmī's works - **spiritual exile** and the **soul's longing for its divine origin,** in the spirit of his metaphysical introspections:

تمام روز در این راز می‌گردد اندیشه‌ام
و شب که فرا می‌رسد، آن را با نفس می‌گویم
از چه سرچشمهٔ مقدسی آمده‌ام؟
کدام کار مقدس مرا فرا می‌خواند؟
در نادانی سرگردانم
روحم بیگانه‌ای‌ست از دیاری دور
این حقیقت در ژرفای من حک شده است
و روزی به آن خانهٔ دور، سفرم باز خواهد گشت

"Tamām-e rūz dar īn rāz mīgardad andīshe-am
Va shab keh farā mīrasad, ān rā bā nafas mīgūyam
Az cheh sarchashmeh-ye muqaddasī āmade-am?
Kadām kār-e muqaddas marā farā mīkhānad?
Dar nādānī sargardānam
Rūham bīgāneh'īst az diyārī dūr

HEART STORY

Īn ḥaqīqat dar jarfā-ye man ḥakk shudeh ast
Va rūzī beh ān khāneh-ye dūr, safaram bāz khāhad gasht"

> *"All day long, my thoughts circle this mystery,*
> *and when night falls, I breathe it aloud.*
> *From what sacred source have I emerged?*
> *What sacred task beckons me forth?*
> *I wander lost in the unknown.*
> *My soul is a stranger from a distant realm—*
> *this truth is etched deep—*
> *and to that faraway home,*
> *my journey will one day return."*

Rūmī

«چون نیک نگه کنی به خود، از غیر ندانی شدن
این نیست تن‌ات، ای پسر، این روح توست از آن‌جهان»

"Chūn nīk nigah kunī beh khod, az ghayr nadānī shudan
Īn nīst tan-at, ey pesar, īn rūḥ-e to'st az ān jahān"

> *"Look closely at yourself,*
> *and you will not think you're from here;*
> *This body is not your essence, my son—*
> *your soul is from that other world."*

Rūmī

این شور ز میخانه پنهانی‌ست
چون باز رسم، باده‌اش نوشم به آسانی‌ست
اکنون چو پرنده‌ای بی‌قرارم
در قفسی زرین، ز دیاری دگرم
روزی رسد که بال گشایم
لیک کیست این که اکنون در گوشم سراید؟
که می‌شنود آواز نهانم؟
و کیست که لب خاموشم را زبان دهد؟

"Īn shūr ze maykhāne-ye pīnhānī-st
Chūn bāz rasam, bāde'ash nūsham be āsānī-st
Aknūn cho parande'ī bī-qarāram
Dar qafasī zarīn, ze dīyārī digaram
Rūzī rasad ke bāl gushāyam
Līk kīst īn ke aknūn dar gūsham sarāyad?
Ke mī-shenavad āvāz-e nihānam?
Va kīst ke lab-e khāmūsham rā zabān dahad?"

"This ecstasy was born
in a distant, hidden tavern.
When I return there,
I shall stand sober and clear.
For now, I am but a restless bird
from a foreign land, trapped within these gilded bars.
The day will come when I soar free again,
yet who whispers now within my ear,
hearing my secret song?
Who lends voice to my silent mouth?"

Rūmī

این شعر
بی نقشه و بی پیش‌اندیشی می‌گشاید
چون از کلام گام می‌گذارم،
سکوتی ژرف مرا دربرمی‌گیرد،
و تنها گاهی سخن می‌گویم،
تنها وقتی که دل فرمان می‌دهد

"īn shi'r—
bī naqšé va bī pīšandīšī mīgōšāyad.
čūn az kalām gāham mīgōzar-am,
sokūtī zard marā darbargīrad,
va tanhā gāhī sokan mīgūyam,
tanhā vīqtī kē del farmān mīdahad."

"This poetry—
it unfolds without plan or forethought.
When I step beyond words,
a profound silence envelops me,
and I speak but rarely,
only when the heart commands."

Rūmī

Rūmī's legacy is a spiritual symphony composed of poetic ecstasy, metaphysical depth, and pedagogical clarity. His works, through diverse translations and commentaries, continue to speak across centuries—nourishing the soul, challenging the intellect, and dissolving the self in the flame of love. Whether read through the lens of rigorous academia, contemporary spiritual accessibility or historical analysis, Rūmī emerges not merely as a poet or mystic, but as a timeless **voice of the human spirit yearning for the divine.** At the heart of **Rūmī's corpus**—especially the *Masnavi*, *Divan-e-Shams*, *Fihi Ma Fihi*, and *Rubaiyat*—is the mystical concept of **Divine Love** as the origin, path, and destination of the human soul. The *Masnavi* presents an encyclopedic view of Sufi metaphysics through parables, allegories, and moral stories. The *Divan-e-Shams* expresses ecstatic union and longing for the Beloved, reflecting Rūmī's spiritual transformation after meeting Shams of Tabriz. *Fihi Ma Fihi*, his discourses, presents a more didactic, philosophical voice, offering spiritual instruction grounded in everyday examples. To get an in-depth understanding of Rūmī's life, his message of altruistic behavior, passionate love of the Divine, and relevance to modern civilization you may read my work, *"Rūmī Soul Healer".*

Heart Story shows us a human journey that is complimented in detail in my lifetime's work, Heart Intelligence – Book and Film. I wrote Heart Story in an attempt to paint a vivid, lively and transcendental narrative that anyone can easily visualize and moreover emancipate its significance for interfaith understanding and coexistence. There are moments in this story when a sense of the Divine invades our intellect and rips it apart to access our hearts and see an inward truth that has no common parallel in the world of the senses - Bon Voyage…

Chapter 1: The Blundering Fanatic

Alpha represents the modern-day manifestation of archaic fanaticism, reconstituted through religious absolutism and tribal nationalism. He is not merely a misguided individual, but a psychological construct shaped by authoritarian religiosity and socio-political conditioning. His worldview is shaped by a binary moral compass—dividing the world into "us" and "them"—that leaves no room for plurality, nuance, or empathy. In this closed system of belief, inherited dogma trumps ethical reasoning, and faith is weaponized as a tool of domination rather than a path to spiritual elevation (Altemeyer & Hunsberger, 2005).

Alpha's behavior exemplifies what Sir Muhammad Iqbal critiqued as "dead thought"—religion reduced to lifeless ritual and imitation, devoid of its inner flame. Iqbal believed that the dynamic, creative force of religion was to be found not in blind conformity but in the awakening of the self, or *Khudi*, through divine introspection and intellectual rigor. "The ultimate aim of the ego," Iqbal wrote, "is not to see something, but to be something" (Iqbal, 1930/2013).

HEART STORY

But Alpha's ego is not elevated—it is enslaved to dogma. His inability to reflect spiritually or philosophically renders him incapable of what Iqbal called *ijtihad*—independent reasoning, the antidote to stagnation and fanaticism.

His theology is rigid and reactionary, not transformative. This is antithetical to the mystical vision of Rūmī, who wrote: *"The religion of love is separate from all religions: the lovers of God have no religion but God alone."* Rūmī's ecstatic metaphysics emphasized the universality of divine love over the narrowness of creed. He warned against mistaking the "wine cup" of external dogma for the "wine" of inner realization. Alpha, tragically, clings to the vessel and misses the spirit.

دینِ عشّاق از همه دین‌ها جداست
عشقِ معشوق از همه کس برتر است
عاشقان را ملّت و مذهب خداست
جز خداشان ملّت و مذهب دگر است

Dīn-e ʿushshāq az hame dīn-hā judāst
ʿIshq-e maʿshūq az hame kas bartar ast
ʿĀshiqān rā millat o mazhab Khodāst
Joz Khodā-shān millat o mazhab digar ast

"The religion of love is separate from all religions:
the lovers of God have no religion but God alone."

Rūmī

This verse reflects Rūmī's transcendent view of divine love (ʿishq-e ilāhī) which rises above formal religions and sectarian boundaries. The key term **"millat o mazhab"** (creed and sect) implies formal, institutional religion, which he asserts becomes irrelevant in the direct, intimate experience of God through love.

A **philosophical and spiritual interpretation** of Rūmī's verse, line by line, integrating both his Sufi metaphysics and universalist ethos:

دینِ عشّاق از همه دین‌ها جداست

"Dīn-e ʿushshāq az hame dīn-hā judāst"

"The religion of lovers is apart from all faiths."

Rūmī

Interpretation:

Here, Rūmī draws a radical distinction between conventional religion—structured through rituals, dogmas, and laws—and the path of divine lovers. The *ʿushshāq* (lovers) are those who are so consumed by love for the Divine that they transcend formalism. Their "religion" is not found in mosques, churches, or temples, but in the burning of the heart and the annihilation (*fanāʾ*) of the self in the Beloved.

This echoes the **Sufi doctrine of experiential knowledge (*maʿrifah*)**, where direct union with God supersedes legalistic boundaries. Rūmī is not denouncing religion itself, but rather showing that divine love (*ʿishq-e ḥaqīqī*) is not confined by institutional forms.

عشق معشوق از همه کس برتر است

"ʿIshq-e maʿshūq az hame kas bartar ast"

"Love for the Beloved surpasses all else."

Rūmī

Interpretation:

The *maʿshūq* (Beloved) is God—utterly transcendent yet intimately near. Love for this Beloved becomes the supreme value, higher than all worldly relationships, identities, or allegiances. In this Sufi vision, love is both the path and the destination. It's a cosmic force—echoing Plato's *Eros*, Augustine's *caritas*, and even the Vedantic notion of *prema*—that draws the soul back to its origin.

This line emphasizes **ontological primacy**: that *ʿishq* is the inner thread of the universe, deeper than law (*sharīʿah*), reason (*ʿaql*), or ritual.

عاشقان را ملَّت و مذهب خداست

"ʿĀshiqān rā millat o mazhab Khodāst"

"The creed and faith of lovers is God alone."

Rūmī

Interpretation:

Here Rūmī speaks to **pure monotheism stripped of intermediaries**. For the lovers, God is not merely the object of worship but the very structure of meaning, identity, and belonging. They do not identify themselves with outward religious labels or sects. Their "millah" and "mazhab"—terms typically denoting community and sectarian affiliation—are not tribal or institutional, but God Himself.

This reflects the **Qur'anic phrase**:

وَلِلَّهِ الدِّينُ الْخَالِصُ

"Wa lillāhi ad-dīn al-khāliṣ"

"And to God alone belongs the pure religion"

(Qur'an 39:3)

The Qur'anic verse **"Wa lillāhi al-dīn al-khāliṣ"** (وَلِلَّهِ الدِّينُ الْخَالِصُ), from Surah Az-Zumar (39:3), using the etymological and linguistic insights from **Martin Lings'** and **Edward Lane's Arabic Lexicon**, focusing on the roots, meanings, and contextual implications.

Transliteration

Wa = And / To
lillāhi = to Allah (to God) [preposition + proper noun in genitive case]
ad-dīn = the religion / the way / the judgment
al-khāliṣ = the pure / the sincere / the unadulterated

Translation

"And to Allah alone belongs the pure (or sincere) religion."

Linguistic and Etymological Analysis

a. دِين (Dīn)

- **Root:** د-ي-ن (D-Y-N)
- **Core meaning:** To owe, to be indebted, to submit, to judge.
- **Extended meanings:** Religion, judgment, law, custom, obligation, system of belief, a way of life involving submission and accountability.

In classical Arabic, **dīn** implies an entire system of judgment and obligation that governs a person's relationship with God, the self, and society. It is a comprehensive term that covers faith, practice, and moral law. The Qur'an frequently uses **dīn** to mean religion but also with connotations of submission and accountability.

Lane's lexicon notes that **dīn** involves **repayment of debt**, indicating the idea of a covenant or accountability before God, which religion embodies.

b. خَالِص (Khāliṣ)

- **Root:** خ-ل-ص (Kh-L-Ṣ)
- **Core meaning:** To be pure, sincere,

untainted, free from admixture or impurity.
- **Derivative meanings:** To be free from corruption, to be genuine, sincere, exclusive.

Al-khāliṣ as an adjective means "pure" or "sincere." It emphasizes the quality of the religion as being free from any form of contamination—whether ritualistic, doctrinal, or cultural—that could detract from its original truth and divine origin.

Lane's lexicon states that **khāliṣ** means purified, chosen, genuine, and free from adulteration.

Contextual and Theological Meaning

- The verse asserts **that only God owns the pure and unadulterated religion**.
- This purity implies that all authentic religion must be free from human additions, distortions, or innovations that corrupt its essence.
- In Islamic theology, this is often interpreted as the **Islamic monotheistic faith** being the final, pure religion ordained by God, untainted by polytheism, superstition, or innovation (bid'ah).
- The emphasis is on the **exclusivity** of God's ownership of the true religion, denying legitimacy to other systems that deviate from pure submission to God alone.

Extended Reflection (from lexical roots)

- **Dīn** carries the idea of accountability and debt repayment: Religion is a covenant between humans and God, involving rights and duties.
- **Khāliṣ** suggests that this religion is one that is sincere and uncontaminated by worldly or false influences.
- Thus, **"al-dīn al-khāliṣ"** is not merely a belief system but a pure, sincere path of submission, accountability, and veneration that belongs solely to God.

Parallel Qur'anic Usage

- In the same Surah (39:2-3), the Qur'an distinguishes between those who associate partners with God and those who follow the **dīn al-khāliṣ**.
- This emphasizes the concept of **tawḥīd** (pure monotheism), which is the essence of the pure religion.

HEART STORY

<div align="center">وَلِلَّهِ الدِّينُ الْخَالِصُ "Wa lillāhi ad-dīn al-khāliṣ" "And to God alone belongs the pure religion" (Qur'an 39:3)</div>				
Arabic	Transliteration	Root Letters	Root Meaning	Expanded Meaning
دِين	Dīn	د-ي-ن	To owe, to submit, judgment	Religion, faith, law, obligation
خَالِص	Khāliṣ	خ-ل-ص	To be pure, sincere	Pure, unadulterated, genuine
وَلِلَّهِ	Wa lillāhi		And to God	Ownership exclusive to God

جز خداشان مَلَّت و مذهب دگر است

"Joz Khodā-shān millat o mazhab digar ast"

"Aside from God, they have no creed or sect."

Rūmī

Interpretation:

This closing line negates any substitute for God as the source of spiritual identity. Even the structures that claim to represent God become meaningless when the heart is enflamed by divine love. This is the **Sufi realization of *tawḥīd*** — the absolute oneness of God — not just intellectually, but existentially lived.

Lovers do not divide over doctrine; they dissolve in divine unity. This resonates with the **Perennial Philosophy** shared by mystics across traditions: the deeper one moves toward the sacred center, the more all outward differences vanish.

Summary:

Rūmī's message in this quatrain is timeless: He invites us to a spiritual path beyond dogma, where God is not a concept to be defended, but a reality to be **loved**, **embodied**, and **experienced**. The "religion of love" is the highest, because it *unites*, while formal religion can *divide*.

In the realm of the heart, love is the only law, God is the only identity, and the Beloved is all that is.

Sociologically, Alpha embodies what is known as **parochial altruism** — that encourages in-group loyalty while promoting hostility toward outsiders, often sanctioned by religious or ethnic myths (Choi & Bowles, 2007). This is in total contrast to as opposed to **authentic altruistic behavior**. His community reinforces this dangerous polarity, validating his zealotry through rituals, exclusionary sermons, and reactionary narratives. This groupthink finds empirical support in Irving Janis's theory of **moral suppression** through consensus (Janis, 1972) and **Bandura's** theory of **moral disengagement** (Bandura, 1999). This thematic exploration is also deeply embedded in the philosophical narratives presented in Plato's *Republic*, where he employs powerful allegories such as the **"Allegory of the Cave", "Ship of State"** and **"Ring of Gyges"** to illuminate the ethical and metaphysical dimensions of human nature, governance, and moral choice. These allegories serve as frameworks for understanding the tension between illusion and reality, the ethical challenges of leadership, and the corruptive potential of unchecked power. A contemporary interpretation of these ideas is further elaborated in *"The Book of Wellbeing"*, which draws on Plato's insights using **Socrates' Critical Thinking Methodology** to underscore the importance of self-awareness, justice, and the cultivation of **inner virtue** in the pursuit of a meaningful life (Plato, trans. 2007).

Mark Twain's aphorism—*"Whenever you find yourself on the side of the majority, it is time to pause and reflect"*—warns of such herd-mentality. Alpha, however, fails to reflect. He is galvanized by collective mob-emotionality and blind obedience to religious authority. Following a virulent sermon by a cleric who masks prejudice in piety, Alpha initiates a violent opposition of other religions, tearing apart centuries of peaceful coexistence.

The path away from Alpha requires moral courage, spiritual intelligence, and historical honesty. Alpha's story is a mirror—held not just to individuals but to civilizations.

God, Let's Talk
I Am Thoroughly Confused!
An Aphorismic Dialogue with God

God, "what happens when we meet?"
God's response:
"On first refection your eyes, bloodshot
On second reflection your mind, laughter
On third reflection your heart, ecstatic."

"God, we are all set for a dimensional leap
Do you copy
We are going to communicate
Irrespective of the silence."
God's response:
"I am ready when you are."

"God, what is greatness?"
God's response:
"Greatness is an incremental value
of how small you are
and yet how infinite
your potential is"

HEART STORY

"God, what do you require of me?"
God's response:
"Forget your Mind, you are not your Mind,
Forget your Body, you are not your Body,
Open your Heart,
Fly."

"God, what is it that you want of me."
God's response:
"Nothing that you do not want for yourself."

"God, how do I live?"
God's response:
"Be alive at every moment, live
Be the eye of whatever you are looking at, live
Be the soul of whatever you want to be, live."

"God, what do you want me to be?"
God's response:
"Yourself!"

"God, why is life full of suffering?"
God's response:
"Leave your windows dirty
and you will see dirt wherever you look
Clean your windows
and you will see myriads of colourful dimensions
Kindly keep your windows clean!
Your illusion is your suffering."

"God, why is there so much evil?"
God's response:
"I don't know, you tell me!
I created human beings to make a difference
I said make a difference not put up a fight
Over trivial rights and wrongs!"

"God, Define Evil?"
God's response:
"The process of self-murder
is the greatest source of evil
It's a condition of being psychologically dead
with a morbid fascination for evil
Thus, then evil is simply
the absence of good."

"God, what is the best way to peace?"
God's response:
"Surrender, wonder, awe!"

"God, what does it take to be happy?"
God's response:
"Travel light!"

"God, if you created the universe, who created you?"
God's response:
"That question is an oxymoron
I am not a thing!
I am not and yet I am

You are stuck in a chicken or egg dilemma
Like a fish not knowing the water, it swims in
No worries
Nobody gets it!"

"God, who am I?"
God's response:
"You are my beloved!"

"God, why am I so full of error?"
God's response:
"It's Okay!
You are lovely in all your imperfections
No matter how much you polish the mirror
It will gather dust
I love your stamina."

"God, why is there a heaven and a hell?"
God's response:
"This is not my doing;
You guys create your own heaven or hell!"

"God, if you ask us not to judge,
then why do you judge us?"
God's response:
"I don't, you will be judged by
your own conscience
Please leave me out of it!"

"God, why different religions?"

God's response:
"I am not religious and have
no understanding of religion
Hence, not qualified to answer this one
Please ask the ones who create religions!
However, there are pockets of truth
But you guys have made a fetish out of them
You are stuck in a small pond
Quibbling with your neighbour,
whose pond is bigger
Have you ever considered
taking a plunge in the ocean?"

"God, what's with the rituals, I don't get it"
God's response:
"All roads lead to me
However, there is another way
You may call it the Heart-Way
It's like a detour, but the view is priceless.
Wanna take a ride!"

"God, I want to love you,
but I don't know how?"
God's response:
"Love yourself, your neighbours,
that tree, this dog
Love especially your enemies
And this way you shall learn to love me."

"God, Why the images?"

God's response:
"Men have created me in their own image
And then blamed me for all the images
Shatter the mirrors
Then you may see me in your own heart."

"God, why do you need my prayers?"
God's response:
"Hello, I am free of any wants
You pray hence avoid the
expensive bill to the psychiatrist
Besides the psychiatrist is also clueless
Alternatively, sing with me and that bee,
this waterfall!"

"God, who is in charge?"
God's response:
"Nobody and everybody!"

"God, why the special places of worship?"
God's response:
"Every place is special
Some places the air between the
two worlds is thinner
That place is your heart."

"God, what's the
creation v/s evolution debate?"
God's response:
"Same thing

*One is a metaphor and
the other is what is the "meta" for.
However, we can get right down to it
and co-create."*

*"God, what is intelligence?"
God's response:
"I knew you would ask
Well, there is no such thing as intelligence
Yet people pursue the mirage
However!
You know that I have forged you
in the light of
Heart Intelligence.
Now my dear
It's time to galvanize your spirit
And bring to life this primeval energy
No doubt
It's a pickle!"*

*"God! What is faith?"
God's response:
"A sense of adventure."*

*"God! What is it with the
rewards and punishments?"
God's response:
"The kind of idealism that
folks like you show is
usually not rewarded by the*

pontiffs and oligarchs of this world
they will actually ostracize you
and manipulate the message of unity and well-being
like they did with
Abraham, Moses, Zarathustra, Buddha,
Rama, Mahavira, Nanak, Christ, Muhammad…
Then they will blame it on me!
So much for rewards and punishments!
In all your tumults, I am with you
I will directly help the case as it is a matter of the Heart and the timing couldn't be better!"
My response:
"It's funny, I always believed that
the world is what we make of it
My sincere gratitude for the reassurance."

"God! Is there a resolution between the seemingly endless debate on
Science and Spirituality?"
God's response:
"I don't play dice neither do I follow any laws
Free will and Destiny
Both are predictable
You may get out of it
As Rūmī said:
'Your place is the place of the placeless
The face of the faceless',
Both Science and Spirituality identify me
It's an attempt at a case that is baseless
I am your own voice

Echoing off the walls of
Science and Spirituality
Both are brave attempts at the impossible
It's an adventure without parallels
All is well!"

"God! Why the challenges in my career?"
God's response:
"You are working on a field
that does not exist yet
Which is tantamount to professional suicide
What some people do in life echoes in eternity
Watch out
There is light at the end of the tunnel."

"God! Why are you so misunderstood?"
God's response:
"People make up cultural mythologies
Because they cannot confront the
actual reality
If I was understood
Then there wouldn't be any room for what you call
Heart Intelligence
So let's begin afresh…"

"God! Why are people so fearful?"
God's response:
"I only created Love
Fear is not my doing
Fear is a low energy state of the mind

HEART STORY

It is the opposite of Love
Love is a state of the heart
Love chases away all the fear based
dark alleys of your mind."

"God! Despite clear knowledge
why do people commit to violence?"
God's response:
"Knowledge by itself is of no value
The tyrants are also a victim of their own rage
Knowledge is like a prism, a structure
Wisdom is the light that passes
through a prism
And splits into myriad of colours."

"God! Quantum Consciousness
What does that even mean?"
God's response:
"It is not within the realm of meaning
You need a new language."

"God! What's with the commandments?"
God's response:
"I don't know
These are bizarre ideas
It seems to me that human beings have a knack for
miss-quotation.
Covenant and commandment are
totally different
My covenant is that if you pursue Love

You will not need anything else
That will be all."

"God! Everlasting punishment!
It does not sound like your doing?"
God's response:
"You bet it isn't!
I created everything with Love
People seem to have a fascination
for condemnation
Don't you think I have
better things to do than
registering the scores of your race
and further, sit in judgment
This truly is a pathetic concept
Keep a clean conscience
That is your way to paradise
Localities are symbolic
It's a state of consciousness
Gabriel is it possible for you to
dissolve the concept of God
Let yourself simply be with me
I swear I have never let anyone down
Least of all you
My beloved
Your confusion is because
you are in my presence
This is the price you pay for crossing
the boundaries of
Time and Space

HEART STORY

I plan to take you towards new frontiers
Leave the realm of petty concepts
Drown yourself in me."

"God, I am confused?"
God's response:
"It's okay
It's an ecstatic state."

"God! Why are you so hidden?"
God's response:
"I am hidden, in plain view."

Gabriel Iqbal

Chapter 2: The Accident – An Existential Collision

One unsuspecting afternoon, Alpha finds himself at the convergence of destiny and despair. At a seemingly innocuous roadside junction, he is struck by a car driven recklessly by a zealous youth whose eyes, as described later by witnesses, blazed with unyielding conviction. The youth's fanatical demeanor is later understood to be rooted in ideological indoctrination rather than personal malice—a critical distinction in the pathology of extremism (Juergensmeyer, 2003). Alpha is hospitalized with multiple injuries, including a whiplash injury that, though physically recoverable, initiates a profound metaphysical crisis.

As Alpha recuperates, he roams the sterile corridors of the hospital. His meandering footsteps become metaphors for his spiritual dislocation. What he sees disorients him further: wards saturated with young men wounded by bullets, maimed by ideological warfare, and haunted by psychological torment. Their eyes mirror centuries of unresolved grief.

One night, the attending physician, who seems like a

weary prophet in disguise, observes Alpha and remarks solemnly, *"It wasn't always like this."* The words echo through the hallway like an elegy for a lost civilization. That same night, Alpha witnesses the death of a young man—barely into his twenties—who had suffered a fatal cardiac arrest. He was supposed to marry the following day. The doctor's explanation is jarring: *"This boy was deeply religious. He bore the burden of expecting everyone to conform to his belief system. The stress, the cognitive dissonance, the loneliness—eventually, his body succumbed."* His voice falters. *"His parents are inconsolable. Their grief reverberates like a lament across the ward."*

This encounter unsettles Alpha. Staring at the lifeless body, he is pierced by the blade of recognition—of his complicity in a culture of intolerance, however unintended. His psyche collapses under the weight of unacknowledged guilt and years of dogmatic rigidity. The bitter seeds he may have sown through casual prejudice and uncritical conformity now sprout in his conscience like thorns.

That night, Alpha attempts to end his life through an overdose of sedatives. In that liminal state between consciousness and oblivion, his mind becomes a battleground of unanswerable questions: *Where did the joy vanish from my motherland? What monstrous act sealed our collective hearts?* These questions reflect not merely personal anguish but civilizational trauma—a theme also explored by Sir Muhammad Iqbal, who wrote in *The Reconstruction of Religious Thought in Islam*, *"The ultimate spiritual basis of all life, as conceived by Islam, is eternal and reveals itself in variety and change."* (Iqbal, 1930). Alpha had forgotten this dynamism and paid the price through spiritual paralysis.

As he drifts into unconsciousness, Jung's dictum resonates like a whisper from the abyss: "There is no coming to consciousness without pain." (Jung, 1953)

Alpha is serendipitously rescued by his wife, Snow—a luminous presence who has long been eclipsed by his emotional apathy and patriarchal conditioning. She recounts a dream of an ancient shrine nestled among the ruins of a vineyard in a high mountain valley. In her vision, a voice—neither masculine nor feminine—declared:

"Only with love can we kindle what is essentially common to us all. Close the mind, open the heart—see the light that we all share: the light of being human."

This epiphany recalls the universalist vision of Jalāl al-Dīn Rūmī, who in his *Masnavi-ye Ma'navi* (Spiritual Couplets) writes:

"بیا تا گل برافشانیم و می در ساغر اندازیم"
"فلک را سقف بشکافیم و طرحی نو دراندازیم"

HEART STORY

"Biyā tā gol bar-afshānīm va mī dar sāghar andāzīm
Falak rā soqf beshkāfīm va tarḥī now dar-andāzīm"

> *"Come, let us scatter flowers*
> *and pour the wine of love into the cup;*
> *Let us rend the heavens and create*
> *a new blueprint of the cosmos."*

Rūmī

Rūmī's call is not to escape the world, but to *re-enchant* it through love—a theme echoed by Karen Armstrong (2014), who argues that compassion is the core of all major religious traditions and that "any interpretation of scripture that breeds violence is illegitimate" (p. 29).

Alpha's near-death experience awakens a dormant humility. Emerson's invocation now rings in his mind:

> *"You are constantly invited to be what you are.*
> *Do not seek for things outside of yourself."*

Ralph waldo Emerson

His marriage, long battered by his chauvinistic indifference, now becomes a site of redemption. For the first time, Alpha listens—truly listens—to Snow. He agrees to visit the sacred site she described.

Burdened with the ashes of his own pride, he embarks on a pilgrimage of penance through a long-abandoned path winding into the mountains. Each step is not just physical exertion but metaphysical ascent.

As he nears the ruins of the shrine, memories flood back. He recalls a time when his valley was not divided by creeds and ethnic walls. In those halcyon days, even minor thefts were societal anomalies; mutual trust and shared values anchored the social fabric.

In a Goethean sense, Alpha is enacting a *Bildungsroman*—a journey not merely of recovery, but of *becoming*. As Goethe wrote in *West–Eastern Divan*:

> *"He who knows himself and others will also recognize: Orient and Occident cannot be separated."*
>
> Goethe

Alpha now realizes that the divide he once helped foster—between *us* and *them*, between secular and sacred, between man and woman—was an illusion. His spiritual exile had not been caused by the absence of God, but by his own estrangement from compassion.

*"We are going in circles
and reaching nowhere
To reach would be to begin again
An optical illusion or a real illusion
Perhaps we have already arrived
Drop the act
Live the moment
That's all there was and will be."*

Gabriel Iqbal

Chapter 3: Mystical Journey with Lalla – The Dervish-Woman

Salsabīl

As Alpha ventured into the illusive highlands, he arrived at the edge of a crystalline spring, known in legend as *Sansabil* - a name reminiscent of the symbolic river flowing in paradise (Qur'an 76:18).

According to **Lane's Arabic-English Lexicon**, the word **"Salsabīl"** (سلسبيل) is a composite form, derived from the triliteral root س‑ل‑س (sīn-lām-sīn), which carries the core meanings of being "smooth," "easy," "flowing freely," and "pleasant in movement or speech." The form سَلْسَلَ means "to cause to flow" or "to let glide," and is related to the idea of something being **fluid, graceful, and harmonious** in its motion. The second part, **sabīl** (سَبِيل), is commonly used in the Qur'an to mean a **way, path, or course**, often denoting the "path of God" or a moral-spiritual journey (Lane, 1863, p. 1413).

Thus, *Salsabīl* evokes the image of a **flowing, melodious, and spiritually uplifting spring or pathway**, one that is **easy to approach and nourishing to the soul**, not just the body. It is not merely physical water, but symbolically denotes **divine guidance, ease, and the flow of spiritual insight**.

Qur'anic and Philosophical Context:

In **Sūrah al-Insān (76:18)**, which describes the bliss of the righteous in the Hereafter, the term *Salsabīl* is used to describe a spring in Paradise. According to **G. A. Parwez**, this is not to be understood solely as a literal river, but rather as a symbol of **divine knowledge and spiritual refreshment** that nourishes the human personality in its ideal, evolved form. He interprets *Salsabīl* as a **metaphorical representation of the system of sustenance** in the divine order—one that is **balanced, just, and satisfying** to the human being at every level: physical, intellectual, emotional, and spiritual (Parwez, 1981). Parwez also emphasizes that the Qur'an often uses sensory metaphors—food, drink, gardens—not just for carnal rewards, but to point toward a **higher plane of existence**, where the human soul is nourished by **truth, justice, and connection to the divine law (nizām-e-rabbubiyyah)** (Parwez, 1981, pp. 141–143).

Spiritual and Symbolic Implications:

- The word **'ayn** (spring) in the verse implies a **source**, suggesting that *Salsabīl* is a **source of inner illumination**.
- The term's fluidity (from *salsala*) and connection to a "path" (from *sabīl*) imply that it refers to a **graceful and effortless progression of knowledge and ethical development**.
- **Lane** points to classical Arabic poetry where related terms are used to describe **eloquence and the music of speech**, further indicating that *Salsabīl* may allude to the **beauty of revelation and divine discourse**.

The use of the word *Salsabīl* in **Qur'an 76:18** is a profound metaphor that combines linguistic grace, spiritual nourishment, and philosophical symbolism. It denotes not only a paradisiacal river but a **divine system that sustains and elevates the human self**.

Arabic:

عَيْنًا فِيهَا تُسَمَّىٰ سَلْسَبِيلًا

'Aynan fīhā tusammā Salsabīlā

HEART STORY

*"A spring therein named **Salsabīl**."*

Qur'an 76:18

Linguistic & etymological analysis (from lane's arabic-english lexicon):

Word: عَيْن (ʿAyn)

Root: ع-ي-ن

Meaning:

- Literally: "eye", "spring", or "source".
- Symbolically: The word ʿayn in classical Arabic is polysemous — it may mean:
    - A water spring or fountain (used often in the Qur'an).
    - The "eye" as an organ.
    - Essence or true nature of something.
    - Something precious

Qur'anic implication:

Here, it signifies a **gushing source of water in Paradise**, often interpreted as a symbol of purity, knowledge, or spiritual life.

Word: تُسَمَّى (Tusammā)

Root: س-م-و / س-م-ي

Form II verb (samma) – passive voice here.

Meaning:

- "To be named" or "to be called."
- From the root **s-m-y**: to name, designate, elevate in status.

Etymological insight from Lane:

- From the noun **"ism"** (اسم) – a "name".
- Lane notes that "naming" in classical Arabic implies **essential identity** and **symbolic reality**, not merely a label. It reflects the **inner character** or **spiritual function** of the thing being named.

Word: سَلْسَبِيل (Salsabīl)

Root (speculative): س-ب-ل or س-ل-س + ب-ل-ل

This word is **unique in the Qur'an** and occurs **only once** — making it a **hapax legomenon** (a word used only once in a text corpus).

Lane notes:

- Salsabīl — combining سَلْسَلَة (salsalah) (smooth, flowing) and سَبِيل (sabīl) (path, way).

According to both **Lane's etymological analysis** and **Parwez's philosophical exposition**, *Salsabīl* is not a stagnant reward, but a **flowing and dynamic principle of spiritual evolution**, embodying the Qur'anic ideals of beauty, ease, and alignment with the divine will. This word is **unique in the Qur'an** and occurs **only once** — making it a **hapax legomenon** (a word used only once in a text corpus).

At *Sansabil* Alpha encountered *Lalla*, a luminous, ethereal woman cloaked in the attire of a wandering dervish. Her presence radiated both mystical authority and maternal compassion. Perceiving the weariness etched on Alpha's face, Lalla offered him a leaf wrapped in soft green petals. Alpha hesitated; her faith, unknown to him, triggered his inherited distrust. His apprehension reflected the deeper epistemological bias of many who, raised within rigid boundaries of identity, often recoil from what lies beyond doctrinal familiarity (Armstrong, 2006).

The air shimmered with serenity, and from an unseen realm, a voice echoed with gentle clarity. Despite Alpha's reluctance, Lalla served him water and invited him to inhale the aroma of the herb. The fragrance was arresting—intoxicating yet sacred—as though carrying the very breath of the divine. Sensing Alpha's hesitation, Lalla communicated telepathically, "This herb is a psychosomatic sacrament, revered by Himalayan mystics and Amazonian shamans alike. Known to some as *Ayahuasca*, it is believed to stimulate the *pineal gland*—the radiant 'seat of the soul,' recognized in ancient mystical traditions for its role in human enlightenment" (Strassman, 2001).

In that moment, Lalla's voice, tender yet decreeing, whispered:

> *"Mystical union consists in this:*
> *That you reduce yourself to your unity*
> *in proclaiming the unity of God –*
> *and thus God makes you the witness of yourself."*

Mansur al-Hallaj

Compelled by her words, Alpha drunk the herbal preparation. Its effect was immediate and profound—his vision dissolved into waves of light, his thoughts unspooled into primordial silence. Alpha, once grounded in the rational, was now lifted into a state of mystical intoxication akin to what Rūmī called *"fana fi'l-Haqq"*: the annihilation of the ego in the divine reality:

HEART STORY

بزن در را که باز کند
برخیز که تابان کند
بیفت که برآردت به آسمان
هیچ شو که گرداندت به هر چه جان

"Bazan dar rā ke bāz konad
Berkhīz ke tābān konad
Bīft ke barārat be āsemān
Hīch sho ke gardānat be har che jān"

"Strike the door, and it shall open wide—
Rise, and your soul will blaze like radiant light—
Fall down, and you will be lifted toward the celestial heights—
Embrace utter nothingness,
and be transformed into the essence of all existence."

Rūmī

As Alpha swayed in the trance, Lalla's celestial voice returned:

"Alpha, many like you come to me, hoping to find healing in the external world. But true healing comes only when one turns inward and embraces the forgotten self."

Startled but moved, Alpha asked earnestly, "Lalla, I am searching for the shrine. Tell me where it lies."

Lalla gently shook her head. "There are no shrines

outside you that can reveal what you refuse to see within. But I shall share with you stories—not of places, but of thresholds between worlds."

This mystical dialogue encapsulates a perennial truth underscored by many thinkers. Sir Muhammad Iqbal, in his *Reconstruction of Religious Thought in Islam*, reminds us that the spiritual journey is an inner ascent: "The ideal of the mystic is not merely to see God, but to be one with Him" (Iqbal, 1930/1989, p. 158). Similarly, Goethe, in his *West-östlicher Divan*, admired the Sufi's experiential inwardness, declaring: *"Wer sich selbst und andre kennt, wird auch hier erkennen: Orient und Occident sind nicht mehr zu trennen"* ("He who knows himself and others will also see that the East and West are no longer separable") (Goethe, 1819/2006).

In the sacred presence of Lalla, Alpha begins to unlearn the dualities that shaped his worldview. He begins to perceive what Karen Armstrong (2009) calls "the god beyond gods" — the ineffable, non-anthropomorphic divine reality that mystics across all traditions have sought not through conquest, but through surrender.

Inner Visions and the Parables of Lalla

Alpha sat motionless by the spring of *Sansabil*, eyes wide yet unseeing, as the elixir coursed through his blood like golden fire. The mountains around him seemed to melt, the air turned into liquid light, and time no longer moved forward but folded into spirals. In this numinous state, Lalla's presence became both infinite and intimate—her form dissolved into ether, yet her voice remained.

"Close your eyes, Alpha. You seek shrines of stone, but the shrine is a flame that burns within."

Lalla's voice guided him deeper into the dreamlike terrain of the soul. The herb had not merely altered his consciousness; it had dismantled the very scaffolding of his ego. What followed were visions— not hallucinations, but sacred parables, narratives projected not by the herb but by his own latent soul.

The Parable of the Mirror

In his vision, Alpha stood before an ancient mirror, cracked and weathered. A voice echoed, "Polish it." As he wiped the grime, his own face slowly emerged—but then faded into a thousand faces: male, female, infant, aged, human, animal, divine. He realized that each was a reflection of one spirit.

تو آیینهٔ رخ الهی هستی
چرا از اینجا به آنجا می‌گردی؟

"To āyīneh-ye rokh-e elāhī hasti
Cherā az īnjā be ānjā migardi?"

"You are the living mirror of the Divine Countenance,
Why do you wander endlessly, seeking from place to place?"

Rūmī

Lalla's voice rang clear again:

"He who sees the many as separate is still blind to the unity behind appearances. The self is not in opposition to the world, but the prism through which God refracts His light."
This echoes Muhammad Iqbal's own vision of selfhood, where **khudi** (self) is not egoism but the **God-reflecting consciousness**—a divine energy actualized through inward growth and struggle (Iqbal, 1930/1989). "The final aim of the ego is not to see something, but to be something," Iqbal wrote. In that moment, Alpha saw that his quest for outer shrines had blinded him to the divine image within.

The Parable of the Forgotten Seed

Next, Alpha saw a barren desert where a dying tree stood. A woman—the spectral form of Lalla—pointed at the roots. "This tree was once a garden, until it forgot the seed." She dropped a single luminous seed into his hand.

As he bent to plant it, the desert began to tremble. The skies opened, rains poured, and the tree blossomed with fruits that sang like birds.

غم مخور، هر چه از دست دادی
دوباره به شکل دیگری بازآید
کودکی که از شیر مادر گرفته‌اند
اکنون شراب و عسل می‌نوشد

"Gham maḵur, har če az dast dādī
Dobāre be šekl-e dīgarī bāzāyad
Kūdakī ke az šīr-e mādar gerefte-and
Aknūn šarāb o 'asal mī-nūšad"

"Grieve not, for all you lose
Returns transformed, reborn anew.
The child once weaned from mother's breast
Now sips the sacred blend of wine and honey."

Rūmī

This story symbolized the **loss and recovery of the inner divine potential**—the seed of spirit buried beneath years of suffering and forgetfulness. It reflects the **Sufi metaphor of the nafs** (lower self) being transformed into the **ruh** (spirit), a motif echoed in the mystical traditions of Christian Gnosticism and Kabbalistic alchemy (Nasr, 2007).

The Parable of the Burning Book

In the final vision, Alpha saw a great library ablaze. Scrolls of sacred knowledge turned to ash, and hermits wept. "Why do they cry?" he asked.

Lalla answered, "Because they memorized the pages but forgot to embody the truth."

From the flames rose a single unburnt book. He opened it: its pages were mirrors, and they reflected him.

This moment evoked Goethe's observation that the divine must be not only read but **lived**:

> *"Was du ererbt von deinen Vätern hast,*
> *Erwirb es, um es zu besitzen."*

> *"What you have inherited from your forefathers,*
> *earn it to make it your own."*

Goethe, Faust I (1808)

It also resonated with Karen Armstrong's (2009) view that religious experience is ultimately performative—not merely the recitation of texts, but the **embodied enactment of compassion, justice, and transcendence**.

As the visions faded, Alpha awoke under the starlit sky beside the spring. Lalla sat quietly, watching him like a mother bird guarding her fledgling.

"You have seen what few dare to see," she said softly. "Now, walk not with fear, but with fire. The shrine you seek is not on the mountain, but in the flame that now burns in your chest."

Alpha bowed his head, tears falling—not of sorrow, but of **recognition**. The journey outward had collapsed inward. In the ancient paradox of the mystics, **he had arrived by disappearing**.

Transformative Wisdom through Mystical Allegory

Sufi Parable of the Pond Fish

One day a fish from a big ocean meets a fish from a small pond. The fish from the small pond tells the fish from the big ocean, "Look at me jumping, and see how wonderful and how deep I can dive". Then the fish from the small pond asks the fish from the big ocean, "Can you now tell me about your jumps and experiences in this so-called ocean of yours". To this, the fish from the big ocean exclaims with a sigh, "I just can't tell you". The fish from the pond asks, "What do you mean?" The fish from the big ocean says, "I can't explain, as I do not have the words for it, you are just so awesome in your pond and my ocean has no dimensions hence I cannot explain". To this, the fish from the pond exclaims, "You should come more often, and I may want to teach you, and then squats like a wound-up toy to take on his next jump in a mighty display of awesomeness!" When the fish from the small pond is exhausted after displaying himself, he says, "You ain't seen nothing yet". To this, the fish from the big ocean tells him, "One day I will take you to the big ocean for yourself to see!"

Explanation:

We limit ourselves with our limited perceptions. If we were to experience new dimensions, we would not be so limited by our self-created world.

Effect on Decision Making:

Our limited mindset fixes us in our own melodrama. Hence, we lose perspective on making better decisions.

> *"Burn worldly love,*
> *rub the ashes and make ink of it,*

*make the heart the pen,
the intellect the writer,
write that which has no end or limit."*

Guru Nanak

*"Teach thy tongue to say 'I do not know,'
and thou shalt progress."*

Moses Maimonides

*"The ocean refuses no river, no river.
The open heart refuses no part of me,
no part of you.
I am one with all that is, one with all;
All that is, is one with me, one with all."*

Sufi Chant

*"I have so many ideas –
that I have no idea anymore...."*

Gabriel Iqbal

The Merchant and the Parrot: The Allegory of Transcendence

This profound tale—treasured by Jalāl ad-Dīn Rūmī—recounts the story of a merchant who caged a parrot. Before traveling to India, he asked the bird if it had a message for its kindred. The parrot requested he convey that he remained imprisoned in a cage, though he relished its apparent delights. Upon hearing this in India, one parrot fell dead in protest, exclaiming, "Behold! This is how we barter our emancipation for illusory pleasures." Witnessing this, the merchant's parrot, upon being told, also collapsed. But to the merchant's astonishment, the parrot revived outside the cage and flew away, revealing the Indian parrot had feigned death—a metaphorical act of renunciation—teaching liberation from self-imposed constraints.

Rūmī's Words:

بمُر که تا بِبینی زندگی را

"Bīmur keh tā bībīnī zindagī rā"

"Die before you die, that you may truly live."

Rūmī

Philosophical Interpretation:

Rūmī's narrative is not merely about escape, but about the metaphysical act of *fanā'*—the annihilation of the ego before physical death. This act reveals divine consciousness. The parrot's 'death' is an allegory of transcendental awakening: true liberation begins with the death of the self. In psychological terms, this parable illustrates the necessity of radical detachment to overcome the prison of sensory gratification and mental conditioning.

Impact on Decision-Making:

True freedom often necessitates spontaneous, intuitive acts of surrender. Detachment from illusion, when done in consciousness, opens the gate to authentic self-realization.

"By this means you will acquire the glory of the whole world."

Hermes Trismegistus, Emerald Tablet

The Farmer's Son: The Reciprocity of Virtue

A humble farmer rescues a wealthy man's child from drowning. Offered a reward, the farmer refuses material compensation. The rich man, instead, offers to sponsor the farmer's son's education. Years later, the farmer's son discovers a cure for a lethal disease, which ultimately saves the rich man's own son.

Philosophical Interpretation:

The parable exemplifies a cornerstone of Sufi ethics:

niyyah (pure intention). The farmer's virtue lies in his disinterest in transactional reciprocity. His sincere action, devoid of ego, returns to him manifold—not in wealth, but in legacy and healing. As Rūmī says:

سازندگی تو از بی‌سوادی‌ست،
یافتن از لطفِ حق، نه از دانشی‌ست.

"Sāzandegī-ye to az bī-sawādī-st,
Yāftan az laṭf-e Ḥaqq, na az dāneshī-st."

"Your power to create is born not of worldly lore,
But from the hidden Grace of the Real—nothing more."
"What you truly find is not through books or schools,
But by the Mercy of God, not the logic of fools."

Rūmī

Impact on Decision-Making:

Decisions rooted in humility and generosity often yield outcomes greater than anticipated. The divine economy rewards virtue in nonlinear, transformative ways.

"Nature is the source of all true knowledge... She has no effect without cause nor invention without necessity."

Leonardo da Vinci

HEART STORY

The Paradox of Ungratefulness

In this poignant tale, a man's son is swept away by the sea. After desperate prayer, a miracle occurs, and the boy returns safely. Yet, the father immediately demands: "But God, where is his jacket?"—highlighting the insidious nature of ingratitude.

Philosophical Interpretation:

The parable reveals a profound spiritual deficiency: the ego's default posture is discontent. Rūmī warns against this blindness:

خریداری نعمت، قیمت می‌خواهد،
ناشکری را بیهوده می‌سازد

*"Kharīdārī-ye ni'mat, qīmat mī-khāhad,
Nā-shukrī rā bīhūda mī-sāzad."*

*"To receive the grace of divine bounty, a cost must be paid—
Ingratitude turns heaven's gifts to dust and waste."*

Or

*"The marketplace of blessings demands the coin of the soul—
Thanklessness bankrupts even the treasures of the unseen."*

Rūmī

Gratitude (*shukr*) in Sufism is not merely an emotion, but a metaphysical posture that aligns the soul with divine harmony.

Impact on Decision-Making:

Gratitude cultivates presence and integrity. It prevents the corruption of the heart by entitlement and expands one's capacity for resilience and grace.

پوشیده باش به ردای سپاس،
که جان تو را از نهان برپاید.

*"Pūshīde bāsh be redā-ye sepās,
ke jān-e to rā az nahān barpāyad."*

*"Drape yourself in the mantle of gratitude,
and watch it nourish the hidden depths of your soul."*

Rūmī

The Hermit and the Fish: The Folly of Ignorant Compassion

In a tragicomic tale, a hermit, thinking it is rescuing a fish, pulls it from water—only to kill it. The hermit laments: "But I only wanted to help."

Philosophical Interpretation:

This parable critiques misguided altruism and anthropocentric logic. Rūmī often denounced intellect divorced from intuitive gnosis:

چون عقل یاری جان نکند
زهر را به جای درمان کند

"Chūn ʿaql yārī-ye jān naknad
Zahr rā beh jā-ye darmān konad"

"When intellect lacks the soul's aid,
It confuses poison for remedy."

Rūmī

The parable is an allegory for technocratic or cultural imperialism—well-intentioned but disastrous interventions due to ignorance of context.

Impact on Decision-Making:

Authentic service demands humility, observation, and awareness of context. Acting without understanding can do more harm than good.

Carrying Your Troubles: The Alchemy of Catharsis

A man burdened by trauma seeks healing from a hermit. The hermit subjects him to a grotesque ritual that ends with the man's own vomit smeared upon him. The hermit explains: "You are disgusted now, but not when you daily carry this filth of memory in your mind."

Philosophical Interpretation:

This parable explores the therapeutic dimensions of shock, catharsis, and ego dissolution. Rūmī proclaims:

نطفه‌ای بودی، بعد شدی خون
آخرین شوی روح، گر بیرون

"Nutfah-ī būdī, ba'd shudī khūn
Ākharīn shavī rūḥ, gar bīrūn"

"You were but a drop—silent, unseen—
Then became blood, pulsing in the stream.
If you break the cage and rise beyond,
At last, you'll be spirit—pure, profound."

Rūmī

Transformation often requires an ego-disrupting event—an ontological rupture that releases latent divine potential. As Carl Jung observed, "Until you make the unconscious conscious, it will direct your life, and you will call it fate."

Impact on Decision-Making:

Letting go of past psychological burdens is essential for experiencing the immediacy of the present. Healing is not gradual alone—it may also erupt through rupture and awakening.

> *"He who knows that enough is enough*
> *will always have enough."*

Lao Tzu

فرشتگان پُر ز نور گردیدند
چو لب گشادند بر ثنا

"Farishtagān pūr z nūr gardīdand,
Chū lab goshaudand bar ṣanā."

"Angels brimmed with radiant light
the moment their lips began to praise."

Rūmī

The Parable of the Movie Star

A renowned film celebrity reunited with a group of childhood companions at a quaint café. During their gathering, the star monopolized the conversation for several hours, passionately narrating anecdotes of personal success and cinematic triumphs. Eventually, he paused and, in a moment of self-reflection, declared: *"Oh, I've monopolized the conversation—please, now tell me, what do you think of me?"*

Philosophical Exegesis:

This anecdote offers a poignant illustration of narcissistic inflation and the limitations it imposes upon personal growth and interpersonal engagement. Those gripped by an exaggerated sense of self are imprisoned by their own conceptual boundaries. They perceive the world not as it is, but as it reflects back upon their own constructed identity. Their moral compass is often dictated by crude binaries—dominated by slogans such as *"might is right"* and *"bigger is better"*—rather than by contemplative discernment or empathetic wisdom.

Implications for Decision-Making:

Such individuals become victims of performative grandeur and public acclaim, unable to transcend the self-constructed echo chambers that insulate them from truth. This pathology is reflected in the hollow façade of celebrity culture. Despite being portrayed as paragons of success within contemporary socio-economic paradigms, many celebrities suffer from profound existential despair. Elevated divorce rates, psychological breakdowns, substance dependence, and even suicides reveal the dark undercurrent beneath the glitter. Fame, then, becomes not a culmination of self-realization, but a spectacular illusion that blinds more than it enlightens. Few escape its dazzling snare.

As Johann Wolfgang von Goethe astutely observed:

"We do not have to visit a madhouse to find disordered minds; our planet is the mental institution of the universe."
Goethe

The Parable of the Tortoise and the Hare

A universally resonant allegory recounts a race between a hare and a tortoise. The hare, confident in its swiftness, sprints ahead and, overcome by hubris, decides to rest mid-race. The tortoise, meanwhile, proceeds with slow yet unwavering determination. Ultimately, the tortoise crosses the finish line first, while the hare remains lost in slumber.

Philosophical Exegesis:

The parable extols the virtue of constancy and measured progress over impetuous acceleration. It cautions against the arrogance of perceived advantage and reminds us that enduring success is often the fruit of patience, discipline, and perseverance.

Implications for Decision-Making:

This principle is vividly manifest in organizational behavior and strategic management. In the corporate world, entities that prioritize strategic foresight, meticulous planning, and long-term stability frequently outperform those driven by reckless ambition or superficial velocity. The adage "slow and steady wins the race" is no cliché—it is a model of sustainable excellence.

Lao Tzu offers a timeless reflection:

> *"Nature does not hurry, yet everything is accomplished."*
> *Lao Tzu*

The Buddha's Refusal to Name the Divine

When Gautama Buddha was asked the perennial

question regarding the nature of God, he responded not with words but with a profound silence. Upon being questioned about his deliberate muteness, the Buddha replied: *"Had I described 'It', people would have fashioned images, rituals, and dogmas around 'It'. Hence, I refrained from labeling the Unnameable."*

Philosophical Exegesis:

Buddha's silence is not evasion but an act of radical transcendence—a refusal to reduce the Infinite to linguistic or conceptual symbols. He recognized that every theological assertion risks becoming idolatry, not just of the physical form but of the abstract concept. Ironically, Buddha's own image is now worshipped in ways that betray his original teachings. This illustrates a universal human tendency: to venerate the form while forgetting the essence.

The essential nature of the Divine—*Brahma, Allah, Yahweh, the Unmoved Mover*—transcends all rituals, creeds, dogmas, and institutions. It is neither object nor idea, but the uncreated essence behind all phenomena.

Buddha distinguished between *Saṃsāra*—the illusory world governed by attachment, desire, and ego—and *Nirvāṇa*, the liberation from illusion. While all spiritual traditions contain parallels to Nirvāṇa, the pure essence is often obfuscated by the noise of institutionalized religion, politicized dogma, economic agendas, and the ever-inflating human ego.

Implications for Decision-Making:

Buddha's ontological silence invites decision-makers—whether spiritual leaders, policy-makers, or ordinary individuals—to surrender ego and conceptual rigidity. It urges a posture of epistemic humility: to seek truth beyond inherited systems of belief without rejecting them altogether. For all authentic traditions, when stripped of their external accretions, converge upon a singular metaphysical core.

Buddha speaks in a transcendent whisper:

> *"There is a state where there is neither earth,*
> *nor water, nor heat, nor air;*
> *neither infinity of space nor*
> *infinity of consciousness,*
> *nor nothingness,*
> *nor perception nor non-perception;*
> *neither this world nor that world,*
> *neither sun nor moon.*
> *It is the Uncreate."*

Buddha

HEART STORY

> *"Only God is essentially real*
> *But not a Thing*
> *Everything else is temporary*
> *Manifest illusion."*
>
> *Gabriel Iqbal*

Albert Einstein, after a lifetime of scientific pursuit, concluded with metaphysical sobriety:

> *"Reality is an illusion, albeit a persistent one."*
>
> *Einstein*

For further elucidation, see *Heart Intelligence*, particularly Chapter 7 and the segment on the double-slit experiment, which explores the quantum illusion of objective reality—a modern echo of ancient metaphysics.

Hallaj on Heart and God:

> *"The beloved does not drink*
> *a single drop of water without seeing*
> *His Face in the cup.*
> *God is He Who flows between*
> *the pericardium and the heart,*
> *just as the tears flow from the eyelids."*

> *"I saw my Lord with the Eye of my heart,*
> *And I said,*
> *"Truly there is no doubt that it is You".*

It is You that I see in everything,
And I do not see You through
anything "but You".

Mansur Al Hallaj

The poem below is by **Bulleh Shah**, a Punjabi Sufi poet, a major mystical figures in Islamic thought. **Bulleh Shah (1680–1757)** was a Punjabi Sufi poet and philosopher from present-day Pakistan.

Original Punjabi (Shahmukhi script – a variant of Urdu)

Title: بوُلّے شاہ: بُلّا! کی جاناں مَیں کون

بُلّا! کی جاناں مَیں کون
نہ مَیں مومن وچ مسیتاں
نہ مَیں وچ کفر دیاں ریتاں
نہ مَیں پاکاں وچ پلیتاں
نہ مَیں موسیٰ نہ فرعون

بُلّا! کی جاناں مَیں کون

نہ مَیں اندر بید کتاباں
نہ مَیں رہندا بھنگ شراباں
نہ مَیں رِندا وچ خراباں
نہ مَیں شاد نہ مَیں غمگین

HEART STORY

بُلا! کی جاناں مَیں کون

نہ مَیں پانی وچ مولا
نہ مَیں آگ نوں چُھہ سکاں
نہ مَیں مٹی نہ مَیں ہوا
نہ مَیں آتش نہ مَیں پون

بُلا! کی جاناں مَیں کون

نہ مَیں عربی نہ لاہوری
نہ مَیں ہندی شہر ناگوری
نہ ہندو نہ ترک پشوری
نہ مَیں رہندا وچ ندوان

بُلا! کی جاناں مَیں کون

نہ مَیں پیدا ناں مَیں مرنا
نہ مَیں وچ پلّی ہور کرنی
نہ مَیں آدم حوّا جنّا
نہ کوئی اپنا ناں ناں

بُلا! کی جاناں مَیں کون

"Bullā! kī jānā̃ ma͠i kaun

'Bullā! kī jānā̃ ma͠i kaun
Na ma͠i mōmin vich masītā̃
Na ma͠i vich kufr diyā̃ rītā̃

Na maĩ pākā̃ vich palītā̃
Na maĩ Mūsā, na Firʿaun

Bullā! kī jānā̃ maĩ kaun

Na maĩ andar Bēd kitābā̃
Na maĩ rahndā bhaṅg sharābā̃
Na maĩ randā̃ vich kharābā̃
Na maĩ shād, na maĩ ghamgīn

Bullā! kī jānā̃ maĩ kaun

Na maĩ pānī vich maulā
Na maĩ āg nū̃ chhu sakā̃
Na maĩ miṭṭī, na maĩ havā
Na maĩ ātish, na maĩ pavann

Bullā! kī jānā̃ maĩ kaun

Na maĩ ʿArabī, na Lāhorī
Na maĩ Hindī shahr Nāgorī
Na Hindu, na Turk Pishorī
Na maĩ rahndā vich Nadāun

Bullā! kī jānā̃ maĩ kaun

Na maĩ paidā, nā maĩ marnā
Na maĩ vich pallī hōr karnī
Na maĩ Ādam Ḥawwā jinnā̃

HEART STORY

Na koī apnā nā nā

Bullā! kī jānā̃ maĩ kaun"

Bullā Doesn't Know Who He Is

"Bulla! I know not who I am
Nor am I a believer of the mosque,
Nor am I in rituals of the infidel
Nor am I the pure inside the impure.
Nor am I inherent in the vedas,
Nor am I present in intoxicants.
Nor am I lost nor the corrupt.
Nor am I union, nor grief,
Nor am I intrinsic in the pure/impure
Nor am I of water, nor of land.
Nor am I fire nor air. Bulla!
I know not who I am
Nor am I Arabic, nor from Lahore,
Nor am I the Indian city of Nagour.
Nor hindu or a turk from Peshawar.
Nor did I create differences of faith,
Nor did I create Adam and Eve
Nor did I name my self.
Beginning or end, I just know the self,
Do not acknowledge duality.
There's none wise than I.
Who is this Bulla shah Bulla!
I know not who I am.

Nor am I Moses, nor Pharoah
Nor am I fire nor wind.
I do not stay in the fabled
Nadaun city (City of Innocents)
Bullashah, who is this man standing?
Bulla! I know not who I am Bulla!
I know not who I am."

Bulleh Shah

This well-known **Sufi poem by Bulleh Shah**, *"Bulla! Ki Jaana Main Kaun"* ("Bulla! I Know Not Who I Am"), is a profound meditation on **identity, self-realization, and the mystical path**. It expresses the Sufi theme of the **annihilation of the ego** and the transcendence of dualities like religion, ethnicity, doctrine, and even the physical elements of creation. Here is a detailed breakdown of the poem's **meaning and symbolism**:

"Bulla! Ki Jaana Main Kaun"

"Bulla! I know not who I am"

This is the refrain. The poet expresses deep **spiritual bewilderment** — a state that arises when the seeker lets go of all labels and identities. It's not ignorance, but **a higher knowing** through unknowing (like the Sufi concept of *fana*, the dissolution of self).

Rejection of Religious Identity

"Na main momin vich masitan / Na main vich kufr diyan reetan"

"I am not a believer in the mosque / Nor do I follow the ways of disbelief"

Bulleh Shah denies association with **organized religion**, both Islamic (*momin*, *masjid*) and un-Islamic (*kufr*), emphasizing that **Truth transcends religious divisions**.

Beyond Purity and Impurity

"Na main pakan vich paleetan"

"I am neither among the pure nor the impure"

He discards moral binaries like purity and impurity, showing that **spiritual identity is beyond external behavior or ritual categories**.

Rejection of Scriptural and Ritual Authority

"Na main andar bed kitaban"

"I am not in the Vedas or scriptures"
Even sacred texts are not the final refuge. For Bulleh, **God is not confined to scriptures**; rather, Divine

truth must be **experienced** directly.

Freedom from Worldly Attachments

"Na main bhang sharaban ch" / "Na main randan vich kharaban"

"I am not in intoxicants / Nor in debauchery or corruption"

Bulleh dismisses both spiritual materialism and worldly pleasures — not denying them, but saying **his essence isn't contained by either**.

Beyond Elements of Nature

"Na main mitti, na main paani / Na main aag, na main hawa"

"I am not of earth, water, fire, or air"

He rejects **material composition** — a powerful allusion to the classical view of the human being as made of four elements. Bulleh says: **his essence is beyond the physical**.

Beyond Ethnic and National Labels

"Na main Arabi, na Lahori / Na main Hindi, Na Nagori"

"I am not Arab, nor from Lahore / Not Indian, not from Nagaur"

Spiritual identity cannot be reduced to **national, linguistic, or ethnic categories.** Bulleh is expressing a **universal self** (*insān-e-kāmil*, perfect human), not bound by geography.

Freedom from Doctrinal Creation Myths

"Na main Adam Hawa da" / "Na koi apna na paraya"

"I am not from Adam or Eve / I have no kin, no stranger"

He rejects even **genealogical or mythological origin stories** — freeing the self from **duality, lineage, and division.**

Mystical Realization

"Bulla! ki jaana main kaun"

"Bulla! I know not who I am"

The refrain comes back as a paradox: though Bulleh **denies every label**, he is **not empty** — he is **full with Being**, the Divine within. This "not knowing" is in fact a **higher knowing** — the spiritual state of unity (*tawḥīd*) beyond ego.

Core Sufi Themes in the Poem:

- **Fana (فناء)** – annihilation of the ego-self.
- **Wahdat al-Wujūd (Unity of Being)** – Consciousness is not separate from the Divine.
- **Ishq-e-Haqiqi** – real love for the Ultimate Truth.
- **Rejection of superficial religiosity** in favor of inner illumination.
- **Universal identity** – transcending culture, nation, and creed.

There is no God – but God and God alone knows and we know not. This then is surrender and then from here on we become co-creators in the divine act of creation. This then is the core value of all religions.

Abraham and the Iconoclasm of Thought: A Metaphysical Parable

In the sacred narrative of Abraham, we encounter not merely a prophet, but a radical metaphysician dismantling the false constructs of divinity. Within the temple of idols, Abraham shatters all but the largest and leaves the axe upon the surviving idol's neck. Confronted by the people and the priests, he simply responds: "Why not ask the one bearing the weapon?" The priests reply, "But these idols cannot speak or act," to which Abraham counters: "Then why do you worship them?"

This incisive dialectic strikes at the heart of religious hypocrisy and logical incoherence. Abraham is persecuted and thrown into the fire, but Divine intervention makes the flames harmless. He walks free—not merely from the fire—but from a civilization entrapped in materialist ritualism and socio-religious hierarchy.

This parable is a timeless metaphor for spiritual discernment, inviting humanity to transcend literalism and embrace the ineffable unity of the Divine.

Mystical Exposition: Rūmī's Iconoclasm Beyond Stone and Concept

Rūmī, the master of spiritual metaphor, extends Abraham's logic to a mystical plane. For him, the true idol is not the stone, but the self, the ego, and the rigid conceptual image of God that imprisons the heart.

هر کسی کو دور ماند از اصل خویش
باز جوید روزگار وصل خویش

"Har kasī kū dūr mānd az aṣl-i khwīsh
Bāz jūyad rūzgār-i waṣl-i khwīsh"

"Every soul that strays from its true origin
Yearns to return to its moment of union."

Rūmī

This yearning for union transcends forms. Rūmī declares that the seeker must go beyond the duality of form and formlessness to encounter the essence:

هر که را اسرار حق آموختند
مهر کردند و دهانش دوختند

"Har ke rā asrār-i ḥaqq āmūkhtand
Muhr kardand u dahānash dūkhtand"

"Whoever was entrusted with Divine secrets—
They sealed his lips, they stitched his mouth."

Rūmī

And when he speaks of vision beyond the physical, he affirms:

چشم را بر بند تا بینی عیان

آنچه ناید در بیان و در بیان

"Chashm rā bar band tā bīnī 'ayān
Ānche nāyad dar bayān ū dar bayan"

"Close your eyes, that you may see clearly
That which eludes all speech and explanation."

Rūmī

These verses elevate Abraham's literal act to a universal principle: truth cannot be confined by physical symbols or intellectual constructs. As Rūmī says:

*بی‌تو دهان بسته شو تا چشم دل بینی
اندر حریف خامی یاری چو آب روان*

"Bī tū dahān basta shū tā chashm-i dil bīnī
Andar ḥarīf-i khāmī yārī chū āb-i rawān"

"Be silent without you [the ego],
so the eye of the heart may open,
In raw adversaries, find a companion like flowing water."

Rūmī

Symbolism, Ego, and Idolatry in All Faiths

The core lesson is not a condemnation of one

religious form over another, but an unveiling of universal human tendencies to absolutize symbols. Whether it is the **Kaʿba**, the **Cross**, or the **Wailing Wall**, these become dangerous only when mistaken for the Divine itself. All major traditions assert that these are symbolic focal points—not objects of worship.

As Goethe wrote in admiration of the East and of Islam's iconoclasm:

> *"Gott ist das Höchste, das über alle Namen hinausgeht."*
> *(God is the Highest, beyond all names.)*
>
> *Goethe*

The Real Idol: Religious Ego and Institutional Power

The real threat lies not in stone idols but in the construction of religious identity that leads to division, hierarchy, and violence. Institutionalized religion often perpetuates a spiritual monopoly, exalting creeds over character and dogma over dialogue. As Iqbal observed:

> *"The ultimate spiritual basis of all life, as conceived by Islam, is eternal and reveals itself in variety and change. A society*

based on such a conception must reconcile, in its life, the categories of permanence and change."

(Iqbal, 1930, The Reconstruction of Religious Thought in Islam)

Rūmī too, rejects all claims to religious superiority, calling all to the door of mercy:

بیا بیا هر چه هستی باز آ
گر کافر و گر بت‌پرستی باز آ
این درگه ما درگه نومیدی نیست
صد بار اگر توبه شکستی باز آ

"Biyā biyā har che hastī bāz ā
Gar kāfir ū gar but-parastī bāz ā
Īn dargah-i mā dargah-i nawmīdī nīst
Ṣad bār agar tawba shikastī bāz ā"

"Come, come, whoever you may be, return!
Be you an infidel or idolater, return!
Our door is not the door of despair—
Even if you've broken your vows a hundred times, return!"

Rūmī

Implications for Ethical Decision-Making

Abraham's story, when filtered through the wisdom of Rūmī, invites us toward **inner iconoclasm**—

breaking not just physical idols, but the false absolutes we hold within:

- Refrain from judgment; cultivate empathy.
- Uphold faith not as pride, but as service to humanity.
- Embrace humility, balance, and ethical action in the world.
- Engage in sustainable and compassionate deeds as true acts of worship.

This is the real test of monotheism—not in declaring there is One God, but in living as though all creation emanates from the One.

Hallaj on God:

> *""Before" does not outstrip God,*
> *"after" does not interrupt God*
> *"of" does not compete with God*
> *for precedence*
> *"from" does not accord with God*
> *"to" does not join with God*
> *"in" does not inhabit God*
> *"when" does not stop God*
> *"if" does not consult with God*
> *"over" does not overshadow God*
> *"under" does not support God*
> *"opposite" does not face God*
> *"with" does not press God*

"behind" does not limit God
"previous" does not display God
"after" does not cause God to pass away
"all" does not unite God
"is" does not bring God into being
"is not" does not deprive God from Being.
Concealment does not veil God
God pre-existence preceded time,
God being preceded non-being
God eternity preceded limit.
If thou sayest 'when',
God existing has outstripped time;
If thou sayest 'before', before is after God;
If thou sayest 'he', 'h' and 'e' are God creation;
If thou sayest 'how',
God essence is veiled from description;
If thou sayest 'where',
God being preceded space;
If thou sayest 'ipseity' (ma huwa),
God's ipseity (huwiwah) is apart from things.
Other than He cannot
be qualified by two (opposite)
qualities at one time;
yet With God they do not create opposition.
God is hidden in God's manifestation,
manifest in God concealing.
God is outward and inward.
near and far; and in this respect God is
removed beyond the resemblance of creation.
God acts without contact,

instructs without meeting,
guides without pointing.
Desires do not conflict with God,
thoughts do not mingle with God:
God's essence is without qualification,
God's action without effort."

Mansur al-Hallaj

Rabia on Seeking God:

"O, my Lord! If I worship
Thee on account of
the fear of Hell,
burn me in Hell,
and if I worship Thee
with the hope of Paradise,
exclude me from it,
but if I worship Thee for Thine own sake,
then withhold not from me
Thine Eternal Beauty."

Rabia Basri

John Lennon on God:

"I believe in God, but not as one thing,
not as an old man in the sky.
I believe that what people call God
is something in all of us.

HEART STORY

*I believe that what
Jesus and Mohammed
and Buddha and all
the rest said was right.
It's just that the
translations have gone wrong."*

John Lennon

*"The appearance of things
changes according to the emotions,
and thus we see magic and beauty in them,
while the magic and beauty are really in ourselves."*

Khalil Gibran

*"Even after all this time,
the sun never says to the earth,
'You owe me.'
Look what happens with a Love like that!
It lights the whole sky."*

Hafiz

"Act, and God will act."

Joan of Arc

*"Abrahim escaped Nimrods fire,
Christ drove them out*

of the temple of Soloman,
Mohammed abolished their manipulation,
They connived to crucify Christ
They crucified and cut
Hallaj into pieces
Burnt Joan of Arc at the stake
Yet they still persist these priests
Dimwitted and sheepish
like a wolf in sheep's clothing."

Gabriel Iqbal

دل هر ذره را که بشکافی
آفتابیش در میان بینی

"Del-e har zarra-rā keh beshkāfī
Āftābīsh dar miyān bīnī"

"Split the heart of every atom,
and you will find the sun shining therein."

Rūmī

This couplet by Jalāl al-Dīn Rūmī (from his *Dīwān-e Shams-e Tabrīzī*) signifies the **luminous potential embedded in each moment and each being**, if only one is attuned to inner clarity. Just as Muhammad illuminated the path through a seemingly mundane act, the *āftāb*—the sun of wisdom—is always available to the heart purified of ego.

Contemporary Cognitive Insight:

This narrative reveals a foundational principle of **collaborative leadership** and **conflict resolution theory**—the movement from **zero-sum frameworks** toward **win-win paradigms**. Solutions often lie not in conquest or concession, but in **mutual elevation**. As George Bernard Shaw aptly observed:

> *"The single biggest problem in communication is the illusion that it has taken place."*
>
> *George Bernard Shaw*

Al-Amīn's approach neutralized illusion by orchestrating **a participatory act of meaning**—transforming a potential war into a shared ritual of unity.

In the words of Einstein:

> *"When the solution is simple, God is answering."*

Indeed, simplicity often lies at the heart of the divine. Al-Amīn's solution, though structurally simple, resonated with profound **spiritual insight** and **psychological precision**—demonstrating that true leadership is not in commanding authority, but in **awakening harmony**.

Implications for Decision-Making:

The story enshrines the value of:

- **Consultative governance (shūrā)** as a mechanism of justice.
- **Consensus-building** as a path to social cohesion.
- **Ethical creativity** as a solution to entrenched conflict.

In moments of high-stakes decision-making, this parable teaches that solutions do not always emerge from logic alone, but from the **intuitive convergence** of heart, wisdom, and humility.

The Native American Parable: "The Wolf I Nourish"

An Indigenous elder from a Native American tradition once conveyed a profound internal moral dialectic, stating: *"Within me reside two wolves—one embodying malevolence and cruelty, the other embodying benevolence and compassion. These two forces are in constant conflict."* When asked which wolf ultimately prevails, the elder paused reflectively and replied, *"The one I choose to feed."*

Interpretive Analysis:

This parable encapsulates a timeless psychological truth: our character is forged through the cumulative effect of our choices. In essence, we do not merely possess habits—they, in turn, possess and shape us. The ethical self is constructed through repeated volitional acts, which gradually crystallize into stable patterns of behavior, be they virtuous or destructive.

Implications for Moral Agency and Decision-Making:

This narrative invites a deeper interrogation of human agency. It underscores the primacy of *self-regulation* and the cultivation of *ethical intentionality*. By consciously reinforcing constructive habits and disciplining destructive impulses, individuals can transform their inner world, thereby altering their outer conduct. The parable implicitly endorses the philosophical imperative to practice *moral vigilance* and *habitual discernment*.

Echoes in Classical Thought:

The axiom *"Know Thyself,"* inscribed at the Temple of Apollo in Delphi, converges meaningfully with the elder's wisdom. It implies that ethical awareness and self-mastery are foundational to human flourishing. Both traditions—Indigenous and Hellenic—articulate a shared metaphysical insight: the soul is a battleground of opposing tendencies, and our conscious alignment with one over the other defines the trajectory of our moral life.

Gabriel's Parable of Creative Design: A Dialectic on Rationality and Transcendence

A symposium of empiricists—self-declared atheists—invited a woman whose grasp extended equally across the epistemic realms of empirical science and spiritual metaphysics. She arrived conspicuously late. When questioned about her delay, she narrated with solemn composure: "While driving, a tempest obstructed my path. As I waited, I witnessed the spontaneous assembly of a jumbo jet—each component flying into place with mathematical precision. It lifted me and delivered me here."

They responded with sardonic laughter: "Surely you do not expect us to believe such nonsense?"

Her tone then shifted—calm yet piercing: "Yet you demand that I believe a vastly more improbable assertion—that the cosmos, governed by intricate constants, stochastic elegance, and lawful symmetry, emerged by accident, devoid of intelligent authorship?"

Silence fell, as minds accustomed to mechanistic paradigms were suddenly confronted with metaphysical vertigo. She concluded, "Call it God, call it Consciousness, or call it the Eternal Principle—but design, dear friends, presupposes a Designer."

She added with contemplative warmth, "The physical sciences may one day reach the periphery of this Mystery, but true comprehension arises not solely through cognition—it requires the synchrony of *Heart Intelligence*."

عقل را دهی رهی به سوختن
قلب را رهی به سوی دیدن است

'Aql rā dahī rahī be sūkhtan
Qalb rā rahī be sū-ye dīdan ast

"Intellect seeks its path in burning inquiry;
The heart seeks its path in unveiled seeing."

Rūmī

Gabriel's Parable of Avoiding Imitation: The Peril of Mimicry

Zee, a seeker of divine truths, resolved to replicate the lives of prophets. He imitated their actions with mechanical precision across decades but found no self-realization. Eventually, broken and despondent, he returned home and renounced his quest. That night, God visited him in a dream:

"Zee, you have not been called to imitation but to

authentic participation. If I had wished to create another prophet, I would have. I created you to be Zee—the kind-hearted, the uniquely gifted."

هر کسی از زن خود شد پیر
نبود پیری ز پیری پیر

"Har kasī az zan-e khod shod pīr
Nabūd pīrī ze pīrī pīr"

"'Each aged himself by echoing others' truths,
But age alone brings not the wisdom of the wise.
                                                                Rūmī

Gabriel's Parable of the Two Brothers and Their Sister: Paths of Knowing

Two brothers pursued different paths—one journeyed the world; the other studied his homeland. Despite accumulating knowledge, both felt a lingering void. Their younger sister, however, served the sick and fed the poor. In her humility and compassion, she needed nothing more.

خدمت خلق راهی به خداست
آنکس که به مردم خدمت کند، به خدا خدمت کرده است

*"Khedmat-e khalq rāhī be Khodāst
Ān kas ke be mardom khedmat konad,
be Khodā khedmat kardeh ast"*

"Service to creation is a gateway to God;
Whoever serves humanity, serves the Divine."

Rūmī

Gabriel's Parable of the Paradox of Truth

A man, tortured by existential dread, sought therapy from psychiatry, science, and theology—none could cure him. Eventually, he turned to blind religiosity and became dogmatic. It was only through **unconditional acts of service** and inward silence that his agony transformed into insight.

من اندیشه را غم از دیدن گیرم
نه از فکر هستی رهی یابم

*"Man andīshe rā gham az dīdan gīram
Na az fekr-e hastī rahī yābam"*

*"My sorrow is born of what I've seen—
Not from the thoughts that circle existence."*

Rūmī

Gabriel's Parable of the Controlling Mother: The Intergenerational Cycle

A mother scolds her daughter for an innocent act. Later, she reveals, "All my life, I was never permitted to pursue what I loved." Her control was the echo of her own suppression.

در خاموشی رنگ راه است
آنکه به نفس راه برد، راه گم کند

"Dar khāmūshī rang-e rāh ast
Ān keh be nafs rāh barad, rāh gom konad"

"In silence lies the color of the path;
He who proceeds by ego alone loses the Way."

Rūmī

He who proceeds by ego alone loses the Way."

Gabriel's Parable of Woman is Creative, Man is Created

After years of abuse and chastisement by many men, a woman had a vision from God. God told her in the vision that woman was created to be "creative," man, on the other hand, is just another "created" being. Men of low moral character will always abuse her as they lust for money, fame, and carnal pleasure. The woman came to recognize her inner strength and embarked on a new chapter as a writer, eventually gaining widespread acclaim. Despite enduring severe poverty and repeated rejection by mainstream publishers, she resolved to establish her own publishing house and took control of her creative destiny.

Explanation:

Women, not men, have been the civilizational wellsprings. Her pain in labor is her wisdom. Art, science, and language all emerged from her capacity for nurturing and expression.

Effect on Decision Making:

A world guided by women might finally offer humanity the chance for harmonious coexistence.

زن پرتوی از جمال حق است
نی آنکه زادۀ مرد است

"Zan partavī az jamāl-e Haqq ast
Nī ān keh zāde-ye mard ast"

"Woman is a radiant beam of God's own beauty—

Not some being born of man."

Rūmī

Gabriel's Parable of Celebrating the Flight of Our Little Bird

In a moment of exhaustion, the narrator reacts with frustration to his children's jubilance—only to learn they were celebrating the recovery of a bird he had rescued. Overcome with emotion, he turns the evening into a joyful celebration.

Explanation:

Live in the present. Pause before reacting. Often, joy hides in the corners of the everyday.

Effect on Decision Making:

Patience is more powerful than judgment. React less, listen more.

اگر بر پر پروانه دستی زنی، نشکند
گر دل شکنی، هزار پروانه بشکند

*"Agar bar par-e parvāneh dastī zanī, nashkanad
Gar del shikanī, hazār parvāneh beshekanad"*

"A butterfly's wing may bear your touch unharmed—
But if you break a heart, a thousand wings will shatter."

Rūmī

Gabriel's Parable of Do Not Live by Other People's Opinions of You

A successful executive dies suddenly. His diary reveals the torment of living under the weight of others' judgments.

Fear of public opinion is a disease. Greatness demands solitude from the noise of the mob.

True leadership means mastering indifference to praise or blame.

تو آن باش که هستی، نه آنچه که خواهند
که صد چهره، صد زخم به جانت نشاند

To ān bāsh keh hastī, na ānche keh khāhand
Keh sad chehreh, sad zakhm be jān-at neshānad

"Be who you are, not what they desire—
For a hundred masks leave a hundred wounds upon your soul."

Rūmī

"God enters into you with all that is his,
as far as you have stripped
yourself of yourself in all things.
It is here that you should begin,
whatever the cost,
for it is here that you will find true peace,
and nowhere else."

Meister Eckhart

"The kingdom of God is within you."

Leo Tolstoy

"Life is beautiful
only if the eyes of the heart are beautiful
It looks almost catastrophic via the mind
Measuring, quibbling and boasting
Let the heart control the mind
and we are off to the next Galaxy
both inward and outward."

Gabriel Iqbal

Overcome by a profound stillness, Alpha gazes at Lalla with a dawning awareness, his eyes reflecting both astonishment and awakening. A gentle, almost incredulous smile forms on his lips as he slowly shakes his head—not in disbelief, but in recognition of a truth too subtle for ordinary speech. "Lalla," he whispers with a reverent breath, "I see now what you meant." In that moment, his consciousness begins to surrender, as the sacred herb—an ancient botanical sacrament long revered by mystics for its capacity to dissolve the veil of illusion—commences its subtle yet potent metamorphic influence.

Like a soul drawn into the luminous corridors of the unseen, Alpha slips into a deep, trance-like sleep. But this is no ordinary slumber; it is an initiatory descent—a symbolic death of the ego—guided by the herb's alkaloidal intelligence. His body lies still, yet inwardly he is in motion, traversing the liminal space between waking reason and sacred vision. The plant's phytochemical essence seems to act not merely on his neurophysiology, but on the very architecture of his inner being, unlocking archetypal memories, ancestral echoes, and the language of the soul.

In surrendering to this altered state, Alpha does not merely sleep—he enters the sanctuary of revelation, a silent temple where the material dissolves and the metaphysical emerges with clarity. It is the first threshold of what Lalla calls *the remembrance of the real*.

> *"Other people's judgments of you*
> *are none of your business.*
> *This then is the acme of a settled heart."*

Gabriel Iqbal

Odes of Solomon

"My heart was split,
and a flower appeared;
and grace sprang up;
and it bore fruit for my God.
You split me, tore my heart open,
illed me with love.
You poured your spirit into me;
I knew you as I know myself.
Speaking waters touched
me from your fountain,
The source of life.
I swallowed them and was drunk
with the water that never dies.
And you have made all things new;
You have shown me all things shining.
You have granted me perfect ease;
I have become like Paradise,
a garden whose fruit is joy;
and you are the sun upon me.
My eyes are radiant with your spirit;
my nostrils fill with your fragrance.
My ears delight in your music,
and my face is covered with your dew.
Blessed are the men and women
who are planted in your garden,
who grow as your trees and flowers grow,
who transform their darkness into light.

HEART STORY

Their roots plunge into darkness;
Their faces turn toward the light.
All those who love you are beautiful;
they overflow with your presence
so that they can do nothing but good.
There is infinite space in your garden;
All men and women are welcome here;
All they need to do is enter."

Odes of Solomon
Ancient Egyptian Papyrus

Chapter 4: Mystical Journey with Lao Tzu – The Inter-Galactic Sage

As dawn breaks over a strange, shimmering horizon, Alpha awakens beneath the emerald veil of a celestial vineyard, nestled in the folds of a dreamscape that defies terrestrial logic. The air carries the scent of distant stars and ancient wisdom. As he rises from the moss-laden earth, Alpha encounters a serene and enigmatic figure—an old man cloaked in flowing robes that seem woven from the light of galaxies. This is Lao Tzu, the legendary philosopher-sage, now reimagined as an *Inter-Galactic Wayfarer*—a cosmic custodian of metaphysical truths.

With a voice trembling from weariness and yearning, Alpha inquires, "Old man, which path leads to the Ancient Shrine—the sanctuary of the Hidden Wisdom?"

Lao Tzu, standing with an unshakable stillness and eyes that mirror aeons of cosmic silence, replies with unerring clarity:

"My son, I am Lao Tzu. There is no such shrine here—at

least not in the way you imagine it."

Lao Tzu

Distressed but undeterred, Alpha lowers his tone and insists with quiet desperation, "I have traversed immense distances—across realms of suffering and revelation—I must find it."

Moved by Alpha's unspoken pain, Lao Tzu gently gestures toward a modest, luminous hut crafted from light and shadow. "Come," he says, "rest in my dwelling. The path you seek cannot be forced—it must be *remembered*."

Inside the ascetic chamber, where time dissolves into a continuum of paradox, Lao Tzu turns to Alpha and poses a penetrating question:

"What compels your search for this mythical shrine?"

Lao Tzu

In response, Alpha unburdens his soul. He narrates his journey through ravaged landscapes of war and greed, through realms both earthly and ethereal, in pursuit of truth, peace, and the primordial memory of divine order.

As the story unfolds, Lao Tzu listens in contemplative silence. Then, with a gaze that pierces beyond the veil of the seen, he extends his hand and places it upon Alpha's chest. In an instant, Alpha's heart ignites—not metaphorically, but viscerally—into a **thundering cosmic resonance**, echoing the rhythm of the Tao itself: the ineffable Way of the Universe.

Startled, Alpha gasps, "Old man! What are you doing?"

But words dissolve as Alpha is drawn into a trance—a luminous state of inner awakening. In this altered consciousness, he does not hear Lao Tzu speak. Instead, he feels the sage's teachings **inscribed directly upon his heart**, transmitted through a pulse older than time.

What follows are not mere parables, but encoded transmissions—symbolic narratives from across dimensions. They whisper of forgotten civilizations, of interstellar harmony, of the Tao flowing through all matter and mind. These stories bypass logic and awaken the deeper intelligence of the soul.

"Old man", Alpha exclaims, "What are you doing?" With this Alpha enters a trance-like state while Lao Tzu communicates the following stories to Alpha's heart:

The River That Remembers

"A river made not of water, but of memory, once flowed across galaxies..."

This vision alludes to **the Tao as the primordial current of existence**, beyond naming or categorization. As Lao Tzu writes:

"The Tao that can be spoken is not the eternal Tao."

(Tao Te Ching, Ch. 1)

The river symbolizes the **unmanifest Source** before human conceptualization. The moment it is "measured" (i.e., intellectually dissected), it is forgotten—a motif echoed by Jalāl ad-Dīn Rūmī, who wrote:

خِرَد را بفروش و حِیرت بخر
که زین بهترت آید اینت هنر

*"Khirad rā bifrūsh o ḥayrat bikhar
Ki zīn bahtar-at āyad īn-at hunar"*

*"Sell your cleverness and buy bewilderment.
This brings you something better—this is your true art."*

Rūmī

In **Jungian terms**, the river is the *unconscious*, and the act of naming represents the ego's intrusion into the Self's wholeness.

The Bird That Would Not Fly

"A bird born with wings of crystal is told not to fly..."

This allegory illustrates **the tragedy of conditioned fear** and **self-limiting belief systems**. The elders represent societal norms that repress the soul's transcendence.
The crystal wings suggest both fragility and perfection—akin to the **al-insān al-kāmil** ((the Self-Realised Human) in Sufi metaphysics, who must break egoic form to achieve divine reflection. Rūmī wrote:

مرغ باغ ملکوتم نیم از عالم خاک
دو سه روزی قفسی ساخته‌اند از بدنم

"Murgh-e bāgh-e malakūtam, na yam az 'ālam-e khāk
Dū-se rūzī qafasī sākhte-and az badanam"

"I am a bird of the celestial garden,
not of the world of dust.
For a few days,

they have made a cage of my body."

Rūmī

In Jungian depth psychology, the bird is an archetype of **spirit and transcendence**, and the fire symbolizes the *process of individuation*—through destruction, the soul attains its true flight.

The Mirror That Refused to Break

"A mirror placed in the void before the universe knew itself..."

This image reflects the **primordial Self**, the **undivided wholeness of the Tao**, prior to fragmentation through multiplicity. As Lao Tzu stated:

> *"Knowing others is intelligence;*
> *knowing yourself is true wisdom."*

(Tao Te Ching, Ch. 33)

The shattering of the mirror by reflections that declare themselves ultimate truths allegorizes **dogma**, **ideological division**, and the fall from unity into duality. It parallels Rūmī's parables:

گر درون قطره‌ای بینی تو بحر بی‌کران
نیست جای شک و گفت، این هست مردانه نظر

"Gar darūn-e qaṯrā'ī bīnī tū baḥr-e bī-karān
Nīst jāy-e shak o goft, īn hast mardāneh naẓar"

If within a drop you can see the boundless sea,
Then there is no doubt—this is a vision of the brave.

Rūmī

This concept appears in many of Rūmī's poems: the **part containing the whole**, *the* **drop symbolizing the ocean**, *or* **the soul mirroring the cosmos**.

تو یکی قطرهٔ بارانی، ولی
در تو بحر بی‌کران پنهان ولی

"Tū yakī qaṯrah-ye bārānī, walī
Dar tū baḥr-e bī-karān penhān walī"

"You are a single drop of rain, yet
Within you lies a hidden boundless sea."

Rūmī

قطرهٔ آبم و دریا شده‌ام
ذره بودم، مه و خورشید و فلق گشته‌ام

HEART STORY

"Qatrah-ye ābam o daryā shude'am
Zarrah būdam, mah o khurshīd o falaq gashtam"

"I was a drop of water, now I've become the sea.
I was a speck,
and now I've turned into the moon,
the sun, and the heavens."

Rūmī

گر نگه داری تو در دل قطره‌ای
صد دریا در وی گنجانی، نه‌ای؟

"Gar nigah dārī tū dar del qatrah'ī
Sad daryā dar vay ganjānī, na'ī?"

"If you truly behold even a single drop within your heart,
Can you not contain a hundred seas in it?"

Rūmī

قطره‌ای هستی، ولی بی‌انتها
از صفات حق ببین اندر خودا

"Qatrah'ī hastī, walī bī-intihā
Az sifāt-e Ḥaqq bebīn andar khudā"

"You are a drop,
yet without end—

*Behold the attributes of
the Truth within yourself."*

Rūmī

Synthesis of the Concept

These verses across Rūmī's corpus form a cohesive metaphysical and mystical doctrine:

- *The **human soul** is not merely a fragment of existence but **contains the whole within**.*
- *The **drop** is a metaphor for the self or the ego, and the **ocean** symbolizes **divine reality**, **universal consciousness**, or **God**.*
- *The path of Sufism involves **realizing this unity** and **transcending egoic boundaries** to awaken the oceanic vastness within.*

The intact mirror at the end signifies the **resilient, unbreakable core of the Self**—what Jung called the *mandala of wholeness*, untouched by the ego's projections.

The Path That Walks Itself

*"Do not seek the path—
for the Tao is not a road,*

it is a pulse…"

Lao Tzu

Here Lao Tzu's core message is distilled: The Tao is not linear or graspable. It is a **non-dual rhythm** of surrender and responsiveness. The idea that the path "walks itself" is a Taoist koan that undoes the very striving to know.

> *"A good traveler has no fixed plans and is not intent on arriving."*
>
> *(Tao Te Ching, Ch. 27)*

The spiral inward, as opposed to forward, suggests **gnosis rather than knowledge**—inner realization over external seeking. Jung described this spiral motion as the *archetypal journey of individuation*, wherein the Self becomes conscious of itself by returning to its center.

Epilogue: The Inner Shrine

Alpha returns from his trance not with new information, but with **an awakened perception**. The shrine he sought never existed "out there." It was always **the chamber of the awakened heart**.

Lao Tzu: *"Now go—be the shrine for others."*

This echoes the Sufi teaching: *"He who knows himself, knows his Lord."*

Alpha, once a seeker of wisdom, becomes its embodiment—a vessel of cosmic remembrance in a forgetful world.

Zen Koan of the Bamboo: The Parable of Delayed Bloom

An elite athlete, after devoting an entire year to rigorous training, returned from the world championships without a single medal. Disheartened, he withdrew from his sport for several years. Upon rekindling his passion, he trained yet again for a year, only to face defeat once more. On a solitary retreat abroad, he encountered a sagacious hermit who perceived the anguish veiled behind his silence. Inviting him for tea in a tranquil garden, the hermit gestured to the towering bamboo and remarked:

"Observe this bamboo—resilient and majestic. For three years it shows no perceptible growth, its vitality concealed beneath the soil. Then, in the fourth year, it soars upward, expanding in both strength and grace."

This allegory awakened the athlete. He committed to

three more years of unyielding discipline. In the fourth year, his resolve was rewarded—he emerged victorious.

Interpretation:

This parable underscores the principle that authentic transformation demands latent incubation. Just as nature obeys unseen rhythms, so too does excellence blossom through patience.

Philosophical Implication:

In decision-making, temporal setbacks must be embraced as gestational phases of greater potential. Mastery is forged not in outcomes, but in unwavering discipline.

"Live your dreams year by year,
Build yourself, like the bamboo,
Invisible first—but destined for magnitude."

Gabriel Iqbal

Zen Koan of the Old Man's Horse: The Dialectic of Fortune and Misfortune

A venerable man and his son lived near the frontier, nurturing a deep kinship with their horses. One day, a horse strayed into foreign lands. Neighbours lamented the misfortune, yet the old man responded serenely, "Who can say what fortune lies within misfortune?"

Months later, the horse returned, accompanied by a magnificent steed. The neighbours now rejoiced, to which the sage repeated, "Who can know what this fortune might yield?"

Subsequently, the son fractured his leg riding the new horse. Again, neighbours grieved; the old man remained unmoved. "Who can say?" he whispered.
Later, war erupted. All able-bodied youth were conscripted—none returned. The son, spared by injury, lived on.

Interpretation:

This narrative encapsulates the Yin-Yang cosmology: reality is a fluid interplay of opposites, where every apparent misfortune may harbor hidden blessings.

Philosophical Implication:

Effective decision-making requires a metacognitive lens, perceiving multiple temporal outcomes instead of immediate binaries of good and bad.

آغازِ هر کاری از انجامِ اوست

HEART STORY

انجام چو دیدی، آغاز آن دان، نکوست

*"Āghāz-e har kārī az anjām-e ūst
Anjām čo dīdī, āghāz ān dān, nekūst"*

*"The beginning of every task is from its end;
When you see the outcome, know that its beginning was good."*

Rūmī

This reflects the notion that the **fruit (outcome)** is the **true initiator**, giving meaning to the **branch (process or means)** — similar to the poetic English rendering you provided.

Zen Koan of the Sound of One Hand Clapping: The Practice of Wu Wei

A master once asked: "When two hands clap, there is sound. What is the sound of one hand?"

This seemingly paradoxical query invokes **Wu Wei**—the Taoist art of non-doing. It is the paradoxical attainment of action through inaction, presence without imposition.

Interpretation:
Stillness, not reaction, reveals truth. Reality emerges

not through forced outcomes but through receptivity.

Philosophical Implication:

Decision-making divorced from attachment to consequence fosters clarity. When action arises from pure awareness, its impact is timeless.

> *"Practice not-doing,*
> *And all shall align."*

Lao Tzu

> *"The seeker of perfection must begin with Logic, then Mathematics, then Physics, and only then ascend to Metaphysics."*

Moses Maimonides

Zen Koan of the Two Hermits: Letting Go of Dogma

Two hermits journeyed across a river. A woman, afraid to cross, sought help. The junior hermit carried her across. Hours later, the senior hermit, disturbed, rebuked him: "We are not to touch women."

The junior replied:

"I left her by the river. You are still carrying her."

Interpretation:

Dogma, when unexamined, imprisons the mind. Presence requires unburdening the psyche of inherited rigidity.

Philosophical Implication:

Freedom in decision-making arises from detachment—not from ethical vacuity, but from contextual morality rooted in awareness.

رازهایشان را درک خواهی کرد،
وقتی که نفس مقدس در درون تو به جنبش آید.

"Rāzhāyishān rā dark khāhī kard,
vaqtī ke nafs-e moqaddas dar darūn-e to be jonbesh āyad."

"You'll understand their secrets,
When sacred breath begins to move within you."

Rūmī

Zen Koan of Finding Wisdom: The Ordeal of Readiness

A zealous young hermit, desperate for enlightenment, repeatedly sought the secret wisdom of a reclusive elder. The old hermit eluded him, until one day, in frustration and anguish, the youth implored for an answer. The elder declared the student unready and invited him to meditate by a forest pond the following day.

Arriving late, the young hermit found the session over. Demanding the secret, the elder forcibly submerged him underwater until he gasped for breath. Pulling him out, the elder softly declared, *"You will seek wisdom only when you desire it as desperately as air itself."*

Interpretation:

True wisdom demands hunger—discipline, patience, and surrender—not impatience or superficial craving.

Philosophical Implication:

Decisions born of desperation or haste lack depth. Only through persistent, deliberate cultivation does understanding emerge.

HEART STORY

هر کسی کو دور ماند از اصل خویش
باز جوید روزگار وصل خویش

Har kasī kū dūr mānd az aṣl-e khwīsh
Bāz jūyad rūzgār-e vasl-e khwīsh

Whoever stays far from their own origin,
Again seeks the time of union with their essence.

Rūmī

This couplet beautifully touches on the idea of veils (distance from origin), interpretation (seeking), and the essence (union) waiting to be realized.

"Rise above sectional interests,
Transcend matter to spirit—
Where unity dwells."

Muhammad Iqbal

Zen Koan of the Teacup: Emptiness as Prerequisite for Learning

A scholar visited a Zen master, inquiring about Zen's nature. The master poured tea until the cup overflowed. The visitor protested, but the master calmly explained:

> *"Like this cup, your mind is full.*
> *To receive Zen, you must first empty it."*

Interpretation:

True learning necessitates unlearning—letting go of preconceptions to receive new truths.

Philosophical Implication:

Decision-making requires deconstruction of entrenched biases. Fresh perspectives arise only from cognitive humility.

> *"Peace dwells not in place,*
> *But in the sanctuary of the soul."*

Marcus Aurelius

Zen Koan of Finding a Piece of the Truth: The Perils of Premature Certainty

Satan approached a meditator who had found a beautifully shaped stone, mistaking it for ultimate Truth. Delighted, the man proclaimed his discovery. Satan lamented:

"Man's folly lies in seizing a fragment and claiming totality."

Interpretation:

Truth is an unfolding journey, not a fixed possession. The desire for certainty risks shallow dogmatism.

Philosophical Implication:

Decision-making must embrace complexity and pluralism rather than premature closure.

عشق بی‌بند و بار،
بی‌ادعا و بی‌مقدار،
هم‌اکنون در بهشت سکونت دارد.

" 'Ishq-e bī-band o bār,
bī-'ad'ā va bī-meqdār,
ham-aknūn dar behesht sokūnat dārad."

"Love untethered,
Without claim or measure,
Dwells already in paradise."

Rūmī

Zen Koan of Is That So: The Power of Equanimity

A revered Zen master faced calumny when falsely accused of fathering a neighbour's child. Responding only, *"Is that so?"* He cared for mother and child without protest. Later, the truth emerged, and villagers sought forgiveness. His reply remained, *"Is that so?"*

Interpretation:

Equanimity in the face of adversity preserves clarity and moral integrity.

Philosophical Implication:

Reactions governed by composure and acceptance enable wiser resolutions than impulsive indignation.

"To love, one must first be patient with what is hated."

Al Ghazali

Zen Koan of Right and Wrong: Compassion Beyond Judgment

An elderly hermit refused to expel a student caught stealing despite demands from others. He reasoned, *"The wise know right and wrong; this poor soul does not. Who else will teach him if I cast him out?"*
The thief's repentance transformed the community.

Interpretation:

True enlightenment transcends simplistic moral binaries; forgiveness nurtures transformation.

Philosophical Implication:

Ethical decisions must balance justice with compassion, recognizing potential for redemption.

> *"I sent my soul through the invisible,*
> *It whispered, 'I am heaven and hell.'"*
> Omar Khayyam

Zen Koan of Nothing Exists: The Limits of Nihilistic Cognition

A student proclaimed the world's emptiness and

denied all phenomena. The elder hermit struck him with a bamboo pipe, then asked, *"If nothing exists, whence your anger?"*

Interpretation:

Intellectual abstractions must be tempered by lived experience; theory divorced from praxis is hollow.

Philosophical Implication:

Decision-making demands humility, avoiding intellectual arrogance detached from reality.

> *"The wise described by many,*
> *Are reflections of our own ideal selves."*
>
> *Ralph Waldo Emerson*

Zen Koan of The Light: Bearing the Lantern

A blind man refused to carry a lantern, indifferent to light or dark. His friend warned that others might stumble into him. Though carrying the lantern, it burnt out before an accident occurred.

Interpretation:

Though one may be personally unaffected by obstacles, awareness of the external world is necessary for harmonious coexistence.

Philosophical Implication:

Decision-making benefits from anticipatory imagination—considering consequences beyond oneself.

> *"Meditation is both means and end."*
>
> *Jiddu Krishnamurti*

Zen Koan of I Don't Know Who I Am But I Am Awake: The Paradox of Identity

Meeting a wanderer, a man asked if he was wizard, warrior, king, messiah, teacher, or God. Each answer was no, until finally the wanderer said, *"I am nothing like that, but I am awake."*

Interpretation:

Selfhood transcends fixed labels; awakening arises from detachment and presence.

Philosophical Implication:

Decision-making unmoored from egoic identifications fosters fluidity and insight.

> *"To a still mind,*
> *The universe surrenders."*

Lao Tzu

Zen Koan of The Other Side: Relativity of Perspective

A traveler seeking a river crossing called to a hermit on the opposite shore. The hermit replied, *"But you are already on the other side."*

Interpretation:

Perspective is relative; the problem and solution often coexist.

Philosophical Implication:

Effective decision-making begins with asking precise questions rather than seeking predetermined answers.

"Concentrate the mind on the present moment."

Buddha

Zen Koan of Doing One Thing at a Time: The Essence of Focus

A hermit said, *"When I sleep, I sleep; when I work, I work; when I eat, I eat."*

His disciples countered that multitasking was necessary. The hermit asked, *"What then of quality?"*

Interpretation:

Singular focus cultivates excellence; fragmented attention sacrifices depth.

Philosophical Implication:

In decision-making, prioritizing quality over quantity yields sustainable outcomes.

"He who chases two rabbits, catches none."

Lao Tzu

Zen Koan of Knowing When Enough Is Enough: The Wisdom of Sufficiency

A student repeatedly failed to heat water due to insufficient firewood. A hermit advised reducing the water volume to match fuel availability. Success followed.

Interpretation:

Restraint and moderation preserve resources and prevent frustration.

Philosophical Implication:

Recognizing limits and practicing sufficiency enhances effective resource management.

Live

"When you are all wasted
by the battles of life
And finally,
given up on ideologies
An embalming hand comes
out of Grace
Race towards it
Hold it
Embrace it

HEART STORY

Cut off your garments
Expose your wounds
Bare your heart
Heal
Forget
Live"

Gabriel Iqbal

Chapter 5: Mystical Journey with Nasrudin – The Witty Metaphysical Doctor

Upon awakening, Alpha discovers himself amidst a verdant glade, where he encounters the renowned Nasrudin, a figure celebrated for his acerbic wit and profound metaphysical insight. Nasrudin fixes Alpha with an intense gaze, as though attempting to pierce through to the very essence of his being. Perplexed, Alpha inquires, "Why do you regard me so?" With a knowing chuckle, Nasrudin replies, "Welcome to a realm where questions and answers alike are rendered futile, save for those inquiries of genuine import—those on which your very existence hinges." Bewildered yet intrigued, Alpha's expression betrays his astonishment. Nasrudin observes, "Ah, that expression is familiar. Let us, then, momentarily set aside your apparent malaise and instead address the root of your disquiet." Thus begins a journey through a series of paradoxical narratives—each a Sufi parable embodying deep metaphysical wisdom.

Nasrudin's Sufi Parable of the Lost Donkey

When informed that his donkey had gone astray, Nasrudin remarked, "Blessedly, I was not mounted upon it, else I too would have been lost."

Exegesis:

Loss, in its truest sense, is experienced only when one's essential self is compromised or forfeited.

Implications for Decision-Making:

Cultivating humor serves as a critical psychological salve, particularly amid adversity and loss.

می‌دانم جان تو خسته است، ای محبوب، برخیز
که این راه بیداری ستاره‌هاست

"Mīdānam jān-e to khaste ast, ey maḥbūb, barkhīz
  Ke īn rāh-e bīdārī-ye setārehāst"

  "I know your soul is weary, beloved, but rise,
    for this path is the awakening of stars."

Rūmī

Nasrudin's Sufi Parable of the Moon's Supremacy over the Sun

Nasrudin once proclaimed in a public assembly, "The moon holds greater utility than the sun." When challenged for justification, he reasoned, "For it is during the night that we most desperately require illumination."

Exegesis:

All value is relative, contingent on context and necessity.

Implications for Decision-Making:

Maintain a balanced appreciation for the seemingly minor or overshadowed, recognizing their essential contributions alongside the obvious or grand.

اشتیاق در جان تو پژواک معشوق است
که تو را به سوی خانه‌اش می‌خواند

*"Ishtiyāq dar jān-e to pajhwāk-e ma'shūq ast
ke to rā be sū-ye khāneh-ash mī-khwānad"*

"The longing in your soul is the echo of the Beloved calling you home."

Rūmī

Nasrudin's Sufi Parable of 'Seeing in the Dark'

Nasrudin proclaimed, "I possess sight in the darkness." A disciple queried, "If so, why then do you carry a candle at night?" Nasrudin responded, "To prevent others from colliding with me."

Exegesis:

Possession of inner knowledge or enlightenment does not guarantee universal awareness. One must remain mindful of others' limitations and needs. Darkness symbolizes absence—of light, of good, of knowledge.

Implications for Decision-Making:

Adopt an attitude of generosity and consideration, presuming others' greater need and vulnerability; such magnanimity enriches the collective journey.

جای زخم همان جاست
که نور در تو وارد می‌شود
از درد خود نگریز،
با شهامت آن را بپذیر
آنچه تو را می‌رنجاند، برکت است
تاریکی شمع توست

*"Jā-ye zakhm hamān jāst
ke nūr dar to vārid mī-shavad*

Az dard-e khod nagrīz,
bā shahāmat ān rā bepazīr
Ānche to rā mī-ranjānad, barakat ast
Tārīkī sham'-e tost"

"The wound is the place
where the Light enters you.
Don't run from your pain—face it with courage.
For what hurts you, blesses you.
Darkness is your candle."

Rūmī

Nasrudin's Sufi Parable of the Father, the Son, and the Donkey

A father and his son were journeying to market with a donkey. Passersby chastised their behavior—first, for not riding; then for the son riding alone; then for the father riding alone; and finally, for overburdening the donkey. Succumbing to public opinion, they ended up carrying the donkey themselves until it slipped and drowned in a river. An elder remarked, "In trying to please all, one ultimately pleases none."

Exegesis:

Efforts to satisfy everyone invariably result in self-defeat and loss.

Implications for Decision-Making:

Wise decisions require inner conviction, independent of external approval; seeking universal validation risks total failure.

گذشته و آینده پرده‌هایی بر رخ حق‌اند؛
بسوزان‌شان، بگذار در آتش بروند.
تا کی می‌گذاری این پاره‌های زودگذر
روحت را چو نی بریده بشکافند؟
تا نی بریده و شکافته بماند،
نه می‌تواند شراب حقایق را بچشد،
نه نفس و بوسه لب‌هایی را که آن را می‌خوانند بازتاب دهد

"Gozashte va āyande parde-hā-yi bar rukh-e ḥaqq-and;
Besūzān-ashān, begozār dar ātaš beravand.
Tā key mīgozārī īn pāre-hā-yi zūdguzar
Rūhat rā chu nī-ye borīde bešekāfand?
Tā nī-ye borīde va šekāfte bemānad,
Na mī-tavānad sharāb-e ḥaqāyeq rā bečšad,
Na nafas va būse-ye lab-hā-yi ī rā ke ān rā mī-xānand bāztāb dahad."

"Past and future are veils drawn across the
Face of the Divine;
Set them ablaze—let them vanish in fire.
How long will you let these fleeting fragments
split your soul like a severed reed?
As long as the reed remains split and sundered,
it cannot taste the wine of hidden truths,

nor echo the breath and kiss of the lips that call it."

Rūmī

Nasrudin's Trial Before the King

Accused of blasphemy by three royal scholars, Nasrudin stood trial. When questioned, Nasrudin posed a seemingly simple query: "What is bread?" The scholars replied differently—bread as sustenance, bread as a physical mixture, bread as divine providence. Nasrudin then asked the king, "How can you place faith in these men who cannot agree on the nature of bread, yet unanimously condemn me?" The king laughed and appointed Nasrudin as his chief councillor.

Exegesis:

Even ostensibly straightforward realities are subject to divergent interpretations. The rush to judgment, especially collective, is fraught with peril.

Implications for Decision-Making:

Embrace multiplicity of perspectives and maintain skepticism of majority consensus absent empirical clarity.

*"Instead of resisting changes, surrender.
Let life be with you, not against you.
If you think 'My life will be
upside down' don't worry.
How do you know down
is not better than upside?"*

Shams Tabrizi

This chapter reveals Nasrudin as an archetype of metaphysical sagacity, whose paradoxes, humor, and wisdom dismantle conventional certainties, inviting the seeker to transcend binary thinking and embrace nuanced, often counterintuitive, truths.

Gardner of Hearts

*"I am a gardener
I plant hearts
I have no other knowledge
No language now
Close the language door and
open the heart portal
Where everything connects as ONE."*

Gabriel Iqbal

Chapter 6: Transcendental Return via Stairway To Heaven

The Dervish-Woman has pacified his restless mind; the Inter-Galactic Sage has soothed the turbulence of his heart; and the Witty Metaphysical Doctor has embalmed his soul with eternal essence. Thus prepared, Alpha stands poised to undertake the culminating phase of his odyssey.

عشق پر زور نہیں ہے یہ وہ آتش غالبؔ
کہ لگائے نہ لگے اور بجھائے نہ بنے

'Ishq par zōr nahī̃ hai yē wuh ātish-e Ghālib
Kē lagā'e na lagē aur bujhā'e na banē

"Love cannot be compelled;
It is an inexhaustible flame—Oh Ghalib,
When it fails to kindle, it remains dormant;
Yet once ignited, it is irrevocably unquenchable."

Ghalib

As Alpha inhales deeply, reclaiming the breath of life, he becomes acutely aware of an unprecedented absence: fear no longer constrains him. With renewed vigor, he quickens his pace until he arrives before a stairway. Adjacent to the initial step, an inscription carved into a weathered rock read: *'Stairway To Heaven'*. Ascending into the mists, he transcends terrestrial boundaries until the delineation between earth and sky dissolves into an ineffable unity.

Suddenly, Rūmī materializes, his voice weaving a lexicon of soulful profundity:

From Rumi's Divān-e Shams

چه تدبیر ای مسلمانان که من خود را نمی‌دانم
نه ترسا و یهودیم نه گبرم نه مسلمانم
نه شرقیم نه غربیم نه بریم نه بحریم
نه ارکان طبیعیم نه از افلاک گردانم
نه از خاکم نه از بادم نه از آبم نه از آتش
نه از عرشم نه از فرشم نه از کونم نه از کانم
نه از هندم نه از چینم نه از بلغار و سقسینم
نه از ملک عراقینم نه از خاک خراسانم
نه از دنیا نه از عقبی نه از جنت نه از دوزخ
نه از آدم نه از حوا نه از فردوس رضوانم
مکانم لا مکان باشد نشانم بی‌نشان باشد
نه تن باشد نه جان باشد که من از جان جانانم
دوی از خود بیرون کرده‌ام یکی دیده‌ام دو عالم را
یکی جویم یکی دانم یکی بینم یکی خوانم
هو الأول هو الآخر هو الظاهر هو الباطن
بغیر از هو و یا من هو دیگر چیزی نمی‌دانم
ز جام عشق سرمستم دو عالم رفت از دستم

بجز رندی و قلاشی نباشد هیچ سامانم
اگر در عمر خود روزی دُمی بی او برآوردم
از آن وقت و از آن ساعت ز عمر خود پشیمانم
اگر در این عزلت دهی دُمی با او مرا
بر هر دو عالم خواهم خندید و خواهم رقصانم
ای شمس تبریزی چنان مستم در این عالم
که جز مستی و قلاشی نباشد هیچ مدامم

"Če tadbīr ey mosalmānān ke man xod-rā namīdānam
Na tarsā va yahūd-am na gabr-am na mosalmān-am
Na šarq-im na ġarb-im na barr-im na baḥr-im
Na arkān-e ṭabī'ī-am na az aflāk-e girdān-am
Na az khāk-am na az bād-am na az āb-am na az ātaš-am
Na az 'arš-am na az farš-am na az kūn-am na az kān-am
Na az Hend-am na az Čīn-am na az Bolġār va Saqsin-am
Na az milk-e 'Irāqīn-am na az khāk-e Xorāsān-am
Na az donyā na az 'aqbi na az jannat na az dozax-am
Na az Ādam na az Ḥavā na az firdaws-e Rizvān-am
Makān-am lā-makān bāšad, nešān-am bī-nešān bāšad
Na tan bāšad na jān bāšad ke man az jān-e jānān-am
Dū'ī az xod bīrūn kardeh-am, yekī dīdeh-am do 'ālam rā
Yekī jovīm yekī dānam, yekī binam yekī xānam
Huwa-l-awwal huwa-l-ākhir, huwa-ẓ-ẓāhir huwa-l-bāṭin
Bigeyr-e Hu wa yā man Hu dīgar čīzī namīdānam
Ze jām-e 'ešq sarmast-am, do 'ālam raft az dast-am
Bejoz-e randidī va qalāšī nabāšad hīč samān-am
Agar dar 'omr-e xod rūzī dūmī bī-ū barāvardam
Az ān vaqt va az ān sā'at ze 'omr-e xod pashīmānam
Agar dar īn 'ozlat dahī dūmī bā Ū marā

Bar har do ʿālam xāham xandid va xāham raqsān-am
Ey Šams-e Tabrīzī, čonān mast-am dar īn ʿālam
Ke joz-e mastī va qalāšī nabāšad hīč modām-am"

"What can I do, O Muslims? I do not know myself.
I am neither Christian, nor Jew, nor Zoroastrian, nor Muslim.
I am not of the East, nor of the West,
Not of the land, nor of the sea.
I am not made of natural elements,
Nor from the revolving spheres above.
I am not of earth, nor air,
Not of fire, nor of water.
I am not of the Throne, nor the Carpet,
Not of the realm of existence or the realm of non-being.
I am not from India, nor from China,
Not from Bulgar, nor from Saqsin.
I am not from the lands of Iraq or Khurasan.
I am not of this world, nor the next,
Not of Paradise, nor of Hell.
I am not of Adam, nor of Eve,
Nor of Eden or Ridwan.
My place is placeless,
My trace is traceless.
I have no body or soul,
For I belong to the soul of the Beloved.
I have cast duality aside,
And seen that the two worlds are one.
I seek One, I know One,
I see One, I call One.
He is the First, He is the Last,

He is the Manifest, He is the Hidden.
Other than Him and the one who is He,
I know nothing.
Drunk with the wine of Love,
I have lost both worlds.
Apart from mischief and ruin,
I have no other concern.
If in my lifetime I ever spent
Even a moment without Him,
From that hour, from that moment,
I regret my life.
If I am granted in solitude
A single moment with Him,
I will laugh at both worlds,
And dance with joy.
O Shams of Tabriz, I am so drunk in this world
That nothing remains of me but drunkenness and ruin."

Rūmī

This mystical declaration of transcendental identity reflects Rumi's ecstatic Sufi annihilation of the ego (fanā') — where the lover melts into the Beloved, beyond all categories of religion, nation, or form.

هر که را نام و نشان بود، بندش کرد
من که نامم ندانم، بنده‌ام آزاد

Har ke rā nām o neshān būd, bandash kard
Man ke nāmam nadānam, bande-am āzād

HEART STORY

*"Whoever has a name and mark, is bound;
But I, who know not my name, am free."*

Rūmī

Alpha is profoundly shaken yet finds within himself a nascent reflective equanimity. Tentatively, he inquires, "Who are you?" Rūmī replies with enigmatic candor, "I am still seeking to know myself; a lifelong quest that remains unfinished. When clarity dawns, I shall share it with you. Until then, trust that your presence here is purposeful."

Inviting Alpha to accompany him into a vineyard, Rūmī leads him through a verdant labyrinth of vines. The intoxicating aroma of ripened grapes suffuses the air, lightening their communion.

"If you came here seeking mere information," Rūmī declares, "I regret to inform you that this sanctuary offers none. For it is information itself that fuels the fanaticism you bear like a burden."

Rūmī probes further, "Why are you here, Alpha?" The seeker admits, "I confess, I do not truly know." Rūmī chuckles, "Yet, when you began, you were certain you knew everything." "Indeed," Alpha concedes. "Ah, a beginning," Rūmī affirms with a knowing smile. "Our affliction," he continues, "is the arrogance of certainty—a veil masking the vast void within our ego. It is only through profound loss and suffering that we recognize the futility of clinging to self-imposed, limiting dogmas. Worse, we sanctify these prisons by invoking divine authority. Our authentic nature, however, is as effortless as a breeze, as unbound as morning dew, and as vital as mountain spring water."

Absorbing these truths, Alpha confesses, "I am utterly bewildered." "Welcome," Rūmī rejoins, "to the fellowship of the mystically confused. The enigma unfolds eternally and therein lies the exquisite charm of confusion—it is the freshness of first love, the spark of awakening. The dogmatic pontiffs seek to extinguish this with their rules and decrees. But souls like yours, wearied by darkness, may yet emerge into the naked self."

در حیرتم از عشق و از آن خلقِ عجیب
هر لحظه مرا تازه کند عشق، طبیب
از خلق گذشتم نه از این عشقِ عجیب
آن لحظه دلم نیست که باشد به فریب

"Dar ḥayratam az ʿishq u az ān khalq-i ʿajīb
Har laḥẓa marā tāza kunad ʿishq, ṭabīb
Az khalq guẕashtam, na az īn ʿishq-i ʿajīb
Ān laḥẓa dilam nīst kih bāshad ba farīb"

"I am bewildered by Love and its wondrous crowd,

HEART STORY

At every moment Love renews me, the true healer.
I have passed beyond creation,
but not beyond this strange Love—
Not for a moment is my heart deceived by illusion."

Rūmī

This quatrain emphasizes **ḥayrat** (حیرت) as a sacred, mystical bewilderment—a state not of confusion, but of awe before the unknowable majesty of Divine Love. Rumi frequently celebrates this bewilderment as a sign of spiritual awakening and annihilation of the ego (**fanā'**).

"My son," Rūmī intones with compassionate warmth, "You embody the very light you seek. No truth surpasses the revelation of your inner self; all else is but noise and disputation. All creation mirrors this yearning — a shared desire to apprehend our essential being. The paradox is simple yet profound: we are all interconnected, and energy is the conduit of this unity. Share it freely, and it multiplies; hoard it, and it stagnates. Cast your heart outward; love returns to you in ever greater abundance. Such is the immutable law of nature."

With a spontaneous whistle, Rūmī bursts into song and begins to whirl. Alpha, seized by an uncanny laughter, joins the ecstatic dance, arms unfurled amid a garden of blooming tulips. Heavenly melodies envelop them. Alpha's movements mimic a butterfly emerging from its cocoon, time dilating as his entire existence unfolds before him in vivid clarity. He perceives, like crystalline spring water, the moments where his soul diverged from truth.

As twilight descends upon the valley, Alpha surrenders to the rhythm of celestial and terrestrial harmonies and collapses into the meadow's embrace. Rūmī, like a nurturing guardian, breathes new spirit into Alpha's soul.

"I am the Alchemist," Rūmī whispers, "a transformer of souls. This land, your land, is fertile and bountiful; it requires only humility and mutual respect for peaceful coexistence. Our bond is energy itself; we thrive only if the forest thrives. Therefore, abide by the golden rule: treat others as you would be treated. Honor the balance with nature and take only what sustains you." With a tender embrace, Rūmī leaves Alpha cradled by the earth's benevolent bosom.

> *"To be yourself in a world that is constantly*
> *trying to make you something else*
> *is the greatest accomplishment."*
>
> *Ralph Waldo Emerson*

Infinitely Beautiful

"Every morning I clean my windows
Every day they get blurred again
I toil quietly to begin again every morning
Fresh with a new song
The world is but a reflection of our perceptions
Mostly skewed!
If we generously polish our windows
The world would appear…
Infinitely beautiful."

Gabriel Iqbal

Chapter 7: Wisdom of the Ages from Shams Tabriz

At the break of dawn, Alpha awakens to the sonorous chorus of innumerable vividly hued birds, whose melodies interweave into a tapestry of natural symphony. Among this vibrant ensemble, a singular voice ascends—slow, deliberate, and imbued with an almost hypnotic cadence: the nightingale's plaintive song. This haunting melody pierces the veil of sleep and stirs within Alpha a profound spiritual yearning. Overwhelmed by the magnitude of the moment, he lifts his gaze to the heavens and casts his arms wide in an act of cathartic surrender, his exhalation a singular, soul-rending cry that echoes across the nascent light.
Snow, whose concern has grown with each passing moment, hastens toward him, her footsteps urgent and filled with the tremulous hope of renewal. She enfolds Alpha in a tender embrace, her voice trembling yet resolute as she implores, "Alpha, shall we not transcend the wounds of the past and commence again, as if reborn...?"

At this juncture, the venerable figure of Rūmī enters, his presence serene yet commanding. With measured gravity, he offers the perennial wisdom inherited from his beloved spiritual companion, Shams Tabriz—the very essence of mystical illumination that transcends epochs and cultures alike:

نه من ماندم نه تو، فقط عشق است
رقص هستی در جویبار هستی است

"Na man māndam na to, faqaṭ ʿeshq ast
Raqṣ-e hastī dar jūybār-e hastī ast"

"Neither I remain nor You, only Love exists,
The dance of being in the stream of existence."

Shams Tabriz

This wisdom, radiant and ineffable, beckons Alpha and Snow toward a transcendent awakening—an invitation to relinquish despair and embrace the boundless potential embedded within the human spirit. Herein lies the alchemy of transformation: through love, surrender, and the dissolution of ego, the soul ascends beyond the temporal, glimpsing the eternal light that animates all creation.

Alpha and Snow are then joined by Rūmī, who offers them the wisdom of the ages from Shams Tabriz:

اول
از موج مشو، خودت موج باش

Az mowj mashav, khodet mowj bāsh

"Do not be carried by the tide—become the tide itself."

or

"Strengthened with active imagery: instead of drifting, you embody the very force of the current."

دوم
آدمِ‌دل پاکِ نجیب، در خلوتِ نفس
عیب دیگران نبیند و شکایتی ندارد

Ādam-del-e pāak-e najīb, dar khalvat-e nafs
'Eybeh digarān nabi'nad va shekāyati nadārad

"A noble, pure-hearted being finds no faults in others and lifts no complaints to the winds."

or

"Echoes inner nobility and quiet strength, heightening the spiritual tone."

سوم
نجاست از درونِ جان برمی‌خیزد
سایر ناپاکی‌ها را آب بزداید
لیک لکه‌ای هست اندر این خلوتِ نور
زهرِ کینه و تنگ‌نظری که روح را زهر می‌کند

HEART STORY

طهارت تن با روزه و ترکِ هوس تحصیل شود
لیکن قلب را جز عشق پاک نمی‌کند

"Najāsat az darun-e jān bar mikhīzad
Sāyer nāpākī-hā rā āb bazdāyad
Lāk lakey-i hast andar in khalvat-e nūr
Zahr-e kīneh o tang-naẓarī ke rūḥ rā zahr mikonad
Tahārat-e tan bā rūẓe o tark-e havas tahsīl shavad
Lēken qalb rā juz 'eshq pāk namīkonad"

"True impurity arises from within the soul;
every other stain can be washed clean.
Yet there is a darkness no purest water can erase:
the venom of hatred and narrow-mindedness.
While fasting and renunciation cleanse the body,
only boundless love can sanctify the heart's secret chamber."

or

"Intensified contrasts emphasize the depth of inner transformation."

چهارم
گذشته تنها سایه‌ای از تعبیر است
و آینده شبحی مبهم
جهان در خطِ زمانی مستقیم از آن‌سو تا این‌جا نمی‌رود
بل از درون و پیرامون‌مان زمان چون مار راه پیماید
ازلی بودن بی‌ساعات سرمد نیست
بلکه بی‌زمان بودن‌ست

تا در پرتو نور ابد غوطه‌ور شوی
گذشته و آینده را رها کن
و روانت را در لحظه‌ی اکنون ثابت کن

"Gozashte tanhā sāye-i az taʿbīr ast
Va āyande shabahi mobham
Jahān dar khat-e zamān-i mostaqīm az ān-sū tā in-jā namī-ravad
Bal az darūn o pīrāmūn-e mā zamān chūn mār rāh peymāyad
Azli būdan bīsāʿāt saramad nīst
Balke bīzamān būdan-ast
Tā dar partow-e nūr-e abad ghotteh-var shawī
Gozashte va āyande rā rahā kon
Va ravānat rā dar lahze-ye aknūn sābet kon"

"The past is but a silhouette of interpretation;
the future, an elusive phantom.
Reality does not march along a straight temporal line—
from then to later—
but time coils through and within us like a serpent.
Eternity is not endless hours, but timelessness itself.
To bathe in the eternal radiance, release past and future, and
anchor your soul firmly in this present moment."

Reworked metaphors (serpent, silhouette) for vivid depth,
stressing the spiritual immediacy of now.

Shams Tabriz

Bibliography

Armstrong, K. (2005). *The Battle for God: A History of Fundamentalism*. Ballantine Books.

Armstrong, K. (2006). *The Great Transformation: The Beginning of Our Religious Traditions*. Knopf.

Armstrong, K. (2009). *The Case for God*. Alfred A. Knopf.

Armstrong, K. (2014). *Fields of blood: Religion and the history of violence*. Knopf.

Barks, C. (2004). *The Essential Rūmī* (New Expanded Edition). HarperOne

Chittick, W. C. (2005). *The Sufi Path of Love: The Spiritual Teachings of Rūmī*. SUNY Press.

Esposito, J. L. (2011). *What Everyone Needs to Know About Islam* (2nd ed.). Oxford University Press.

Goethe, J. W. von. (1819/1998). *West–Eastern Divan* (M. Byrne, Trans.). Suhrkamp/Insel.

Goethe, J. W. von. (1994). *West-östlicher Divan* [West-Eastern Divan]. Princeton University Press. (Original work published 1819)

Goethe, J. W. von. (2006). *Faust I & II* (S. Atkins, Trans.). Suhrkamp. (Original work published 1808)

Goethe, J. W. von. (2006). *West-Eastern Divan* (M. Green, Trans.). Suhrkamp. (Original work published 1819)

Iqbal, Gabriel (2025). Heart Intelligence: *Powerful Self Consciousness*. 10th Anniversary Revised Edition 2024. 1st ed. 2014. Eureka Academy, Canada.

Iqbal, Gabriel (2025). *Illustrated Encyclopedia of Science and Civilization in Islam: The Origins and Sustainable Ethical Applications of Practical Empirical Experimental Scientific Method.*

1st ed. 2015. Eureka Academy, Canada.

Iqbal, M. (1915). *Asrar-e-Khudi* [Secrets of the Self]. Lahore: Sheikh Muhammad Ashraf.

Iqbal, M. (1923). *Payam-e-Mashriq* [Message of the East]. Lahore: Sheikh Muhammad Ashraf.

Iqbal, M. (1924). *Bang-e-Dra* [The Call of the Marching Bell]. Lahore: Sheikh Muhammad Ashraf.

Iqbal, M. (1930). *The Reconstruction of Religious Thought in Islam*. Oxford University Press.

Iqbal, M. (1930). *The Secrets of the Self*. Oxford University Press.

Iqbal, M. (1935). *Bal-e-Jibril* [Gabriel's Wing]. Lahore: Sheikh Muhammad Ashraf.

Iqbal, M. (1936). *Reconstruction of Religious Thought in Islam*. Lahore: Oxford University Press.

Iqbal, M. (1989). *The Reconstruction of Religious Thought in Islam*. Institute of Islamic Culture. (Original work published 1930).

Iqbal, Muhammad (1928). A Plea for the Deeper Study of Muslim Scientists. Delivered at the Fifth Oriental Conference, Lahore, on 20 November 1928.

Iqbal, Muhammad (1989). The Reconstruction of Religious Thought in Islam. Second edition. Edited and Annotated by M. Saeed Sheikh. Iqbal Academy Pakistan, 139-A, New Muslim Town, Lahore and Institute of Islamic Culture, 2-Club Road, Lahore.

Iqbal, Muhammad. (1915). *Asrar-e-Khudi (Secrets of the Self)*. Lahore: Shaikh Ghulam Ali and Sons.

Iqbal, Muhammad. (1924). *Bang-e-Dra (The Call of the Marching Bell)*. Lahore: Iqbal Academy. On November 9, 1877 the Islamic poet-philosopher Allameh Muhammad Iqbal was born. He received early education under the supervision of Moulwi Syed Mir Hasan and won distinctions in Arabic and Persian. Allameh Iqbal passed Middle, Matriculate and Intermediate examinations from Scotch Mission High School/College (now Murray), Sialkot. He graduated the Government college, Lahore, in 1897 and won scholarships and two gold medals in the English and Arabic languages.

After obtaining a Masters Degree in Philosophy in 1899, he taught in the Oriental, Government and Islamia colleges, Lahore. In 1907, he received a Ph.D. degree from Munich University, Germany and the next year, qualified for Bar-at-law from Lincoln's Inn, London. Allameh Iqbal was introduced in Europe through the translation of his Persian work which was rendered into English by Prof. Nicholson. The original work was first published in 1915. It was the beginning of his most productive period and a number of literary works of world-wide repute appeared under the titles: Ramuz-i-Bekhudi (1918, Pyam-i-Mashriq (1923), Ban-i-Dara (1924), Zaburi-i-Ajam (1927), Javed Namah (1932), Bal-i-Jabrell (1935), Zarb-i-Kaleem (1936) and Armghan-i-Hijaz (published post-humously in 1938). These publication brought his name to the greatest heights of fame in poetry, philosophy and political thought. His philosophical position was articulated by his momentous lectures published collectively as "The Reconstruction of Religious Thought in Islam" Read online: http://www.allamaiqbal.com/works/prose/english/reconstruction

Iqbal, Muhammad. Poetic works of Sir Muhammad Iqbal: Asrar-i-Khudi ("The Secrets of the Self")Rumuz-i-Bekhudi ("The Secrets of Selflessness")Payam-i-Mashriq ("Message from the East")Bang-i-Dara ("The Call Of The Marching Bell")Zabur-i-Ajam ("Persian Psalms")Javid NamaBal-i-Jibril ("Gabriel's Wing")Zarb-i-Kalim ("The Rod of the Moses")Pas Chih Bayad Kard ("What Should Then Be Done O People of the East")Armaghan-i-Hijaz ("Gift from Hijaz")Sare Jahan se AcchaLab Pe Aati Hai DuaShikwa and Jawab-e-ShikwaIblees Ki Majlis-e-Shura Read online: http://www.allamaiqbal.com/works/prose/english/reconstruction

Juergensmeyer, M. (2003). *Terror in the Mind of God: The Global Rise of Religious Violence* (3rd ed.). University of California Press.

Juergensmeyer, M. (2003). *Terror in the mind of God: The global rise of religious violence* (3rd ed.). University of California Press.

Jung, C. G. (1953). *Psychology and religion: West and East*. Princeton University Press.

Jung, C. G. (1969). *The Archetypes and the Collective Unconscious*. Princeton University Press.

Jung, C.G. (1959). *Aion: Researches into the Phenomenology of the Self*. Princeton University Press.

Jung, C.G. (1968). *Man and His Symbols*. Dell.

Lane, E. W. (1863). *An Arabic-English Lexicon* (Vol. 1–8). London: Williams and Norgate.

Lao Tzu. (Trans. D.C. Lau, 1963). *Tao Te Ching*. Penguin Classics.

Lao Tzu. *Tao Te Ching*

Lao Tzu. *Tao Te Ching*, Chapter 27.

Nasr, S. H. (1968). *Science and Civilization in Islam*. Harvard University Press.

Nasr, S. H. (1972). *Sufi Essays*. SUNY Press.

Nasr, S. H. (2007). *The Garden of Truth: The Vision and Promise of Sufism, Islam's Mystical Tradition*. HarperOne.

Nicholson, R. A. (Trans.). (1925). *The Mathnawí of Jalálu'ddín Rúmí*. E. J. W. Gibb Memorial Series.

Nicholson, R. A. (Trans.). (1926). *Selected Poems from the Divan-e Shams-e Tabrizi by Jalal al-Din Rūmī*. Cambridge University Press.

Parwez, G. A. (1981). *Exposition of the Holy Qur'an*. Lahore: Tolu-e-Islam Trust.

Plato, *The Republic*, Translated by Benjamin Jowett, Release Date: October, 1998 [eBook #1497]

Plato. (1997). Complete Works (J. M. Cooper & D. S. Hutchinson, Eds.). Hackett Publishing.

Plato. (1997). The Republic (G. M. A. Grube and C. D. C. Reeve, Trans.). Hackett Publishing.

Plato. (2000). *Phaedo* (G. M. A. Grube, Trans.). Hackett Publishing Company.

Plato. (2007). *The Republic* (D. Lee, Trans.; 2nd ed.). Penguin

Classics. (Original work published ca. 380 BCE)

Plato. (380 BCE). The Republic.

Rūmī Rules. Time. 2002-09-29. Retrieved 2014-04-22.

Rūmī, *Divan-e-Shams*, translated by Kabir Helminski, 2003.

Rūmī, *Fihi Ma Fihi*, translated by Kabir Helminski, 2004.

Rūmī, J. (1998). *Fihi Ma Fihi (Discourses of Rūmī)* (A. J. Arberry, Trans.). Routledge.

Rūmī, J. (2004). *The Essential Rūmī* (Coleman Barks, Trans.). HarperOne. (Original work 13th century)

Rūmī, J. (2004-2008). *The Masnavi: Book One* (translated by J. Mojaddedi). Oxford University Press.

Rūmī, J. (*Masnavi*). Translations from R.A. Nicholson, 1925-1940. London: Luzac and Co. Rūmī, Jalal al-Din. (1258). *Masnavi-i Ma'navi*.

Rūmī, J. (Trans. Coleman Barks, 1995). *The Essential Rūmī*. HarperOne.

Rūmī, J. A. D. (2007). *The Masnavi, Book One* (J. Mojaddedi, Trans.). Oxford University Press.

Rūmī, J. *Divan-e Shams-e Tabrizi* (Latin transliteration: Dīvān-e Šams-e Tabrīzī).

Rūmī, J. *Fihi Ma Fihi* (Discourses of Rūmī).

Rūmī, *Mathnawi*, translated by E.H. Whinfield, 1898.

Rūmī. (1995). *Masnavi* (A. J. Arberry, Trans.). In *The Essential Rūmī*. HarperOne.

Rūmī: 53 Secrets from the Tavern of Love: Poems from the Rubaiyat of Mowlana Rūmī, translated by Amin Banani and Anthony A. Lee (White Cloud Press, 2014)

RŪMĪ: His Teachings And Philosophy by R.M. Chopra, Iran Society, Kolkata (2007).

Rūmī: The Path of Love, by Manuela Dunn Mascetti (Editor) Camille and Kabir Helminski, Hardcover - 96 pages (4 November, 1999) Element Books Ltd

Rūmī's Divan of Shems of Tabriz Selected Odes (Element Classics of World Spirituality) Mevlana Jalaluddin Rūmī, et al / Published 1997.

Rūmī's Thoughts, edited by Seyed G Safavi, London: London

Academy of Iranian Studies, 2003.
Schimmel, A. (1975). *Mystical Dimensions of Islam*. University of North Carolina Press.
Schimmel, A. (1975). *Mystical Dimensions of Islam*. University of North Carolina Press.
Schimmel, A. (1975). *Mystical Dimensions of Islam*. University of North Carolina Press.
Strassman, R. (2001). *DMT: The Spirit Molecule*. Park Street Press.

Publications by the Author

Books and Films

Heart Intelligence Film. A non-profit enterprise for public education. 2014. Eureka Academy, Canada.
Available on: www.heartintelligencebook.com

Heart Intelligence: Powerful Self Consciousness. 2014 1st Edition. 10th Anniversary Revised Edition 2024. Eureka Academy, Canada.

Heart Story: A Metamorphic Odyssey into the Heart of Human Consciousness. 2014 1st Edition. 10th Anniversary Revised Edition 2024. Eureka Academy, Canada.

Illustrated Encyclopedia of Science and Civilisation in Islam: The Origins and Sustainable Ethical Applications of Practical Empirical Experimental Scientific Method. 2015 1st Edition. 10th Anniversary Revised Edition 2025. Eureka Academy, Canada.

Rūmī Soul Healer: A Transcendental Story of Ecstatic Passion and Mystical Love. 2015 1st Edition. 10th Anniversary Revised Edition 2025.

Eureka Academy, Canada.

Transcending on the Wings of Gabriel: Collected Metaphysical Aphorisms of Gabriel Iqbal. 2014 1st Edition. 10th Anniversary Revised Edition 2025. Eureka Academy, Canada.

TOYOTA Illustrated Encyclopedia of Lean Management: An Internationally Proven Practical Step by Step Training Manual For Creating a Culture of Powerful Proactive Organizational Effectiveness, Business Success and Sustainability. Kaizen, 5S System, Total Quality Management, Just In Time, Pull System, Poka-Yoke, Kanban, Muda, Mura, Muri, Jidoka, Gemba... 2015 1st Edition. 10th Anniversary Revised Edition 2025. Eureka Academy, Canada.

The Book of Wellbeing: As Above, So Below, As Within, So Without. 2025. Eureka Academy, Canada.

Heart-Powered AI Stewardship: Heart Intelligence as a Pragmatic Solution for Navigating the Existential Challenges of Artificial Intelligence. 2025. Eureka Academy, Canada.

Rūmī's Reed Flute Poem: Transliteration, English Translation and Explanation by Gabriel

Iqbal from the Original Poem in Persian. 2015 1ˢᵗ Edition. 10ᵗʰ Anniversary Revised Edition 2025. Eureka Academy, Canada.

Terminating Diseases by Targeting Root Causes: Synergizing Ivermectin, Fenbendazole, Methylene Blue to Kill Parasites and Restore Mitochondrial Health Using Anti-inflammatory Nutrition and Alkalization. 2025. Eureka Academy, Canada.

GABRIEL'S TRANSDISCIPLINARY FRAMEWORK FOR WORLD PEACE: Applying Universal Altruistic Principles from Religion, Spirituality, and Science for World Peace, Human Upliftment, and Sustainable Wellbeing. 2025. Eureka Academy, Canada.

Environmental Research Publications

Energy Efficiency Global Challenges and Solutions. 1996. Study conducted with students from Carlton Bolling College, Bradford, UK

Fresh Water Ecology and Cultural Eutrophication. 1996. Study conducted with students from Carlton Bolling College, Bradford, UK

The Effect's of Human Impact on Biodiversity. 1996.

A study conducted with students from Thomas Danby College, Leeds, UK.

Project SFFF (Save Flora and Fauna of Fujairah). 1997. Research conducted for Fujairah Municipality, UAE

How do we Deal with the Environmental Catastrophe Facing Kashmir? Model: How to Save Dal and Nageen Lake 1997

A Guide to Research the Mangrove Ecology and Environmental Degradation of Khor Kalba Mangrove. Study conducted with students from Our Own English High School, UAE. 1997

Blue Whales 1st ed. 2000. 2nd ed.2004

Human Population Dynamics: Population Growth and the Environment. 2007 Research conducted in association with students from Shanghai University.

Environmental and Social Responsibility. 2008

Vision 2050 A Dialogue on Sustainability. 2009. The Middle Eastern Perspective World Business Council on Sustainable Development List of Contributors

Sustainable Development and the Stewardship Ethic. Part 1. 2009

Sustainable Development and the Stewardship Ethic. Part 2. 2010

Energy Saving Ideas and Strategies. 2010

Environmental Management Systems Awareness Training. 2011 ISO 14001 and OHSAS 18001

Save Electricity, Save Money, Save the Earth. 2012

Effective Change Management for a Practical Environmental Campaign. 2012

Investigating the Impact of a Colony of Double-Crested Cormorants on the Surrounding Ecological Niche of Hickory Island, Cootes Paradise. 2012

Biological Lessons in Coexistence. 2013

Educational Methodology Models: 2014
Reductionist, Wholistic or Sustainable Model

Leadership Development Research Publications

21st Century Leadership Paradigm Shift. 2008

Effective Management Principles. 2008

Strategic Recruitment Planning. 2008

Leadership and Perception Challenge. 2008

Powerful Well Being. 2008

Live Now. 2008

Team Building Games. 2008

Effective Management and Succession Planning. 2009

Effective Presentation Skills. 2009

Strategic Marketing Plan. 2009

5S System - Workshop. 2012

Professional Etiquette. 2012

Online publications by the author are available on:

www.eurekamakingadifference.com/research-publications

Customer Review

As a token of your appreciation,
we welcome you to write a review on
Amazon

Amazon link:

www.amazon.com/Gabriel-Iqbal/e/B00PTJ0OIK

Customer reviews are important and we sincerely request a courteous review if you are inspired by the author's work and its value for the emancipation of humanity.

Thank you.

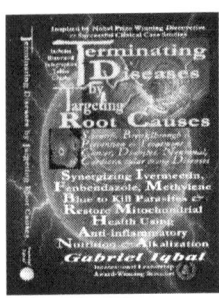

The author is offering this book for free due to his concern for overcoming the worldwide exponential increase in various diseases. To download a free digital copy visit:
www.gabrieliqbal.com

TERMINATING DISEASES BY TARGETING ROOT CAUSES
Film Documentary - Preview of the Book
Available for viewing at no cost as a public education enterprise on:

www.gabrieliqbal.com

or

https://www.youtube.com/watch?v=Kd1QDCNU-gw&t=1s

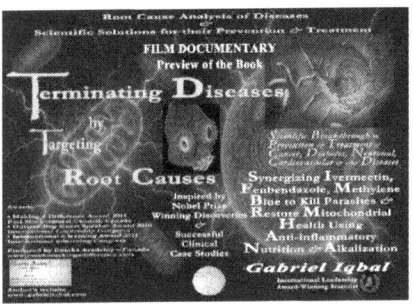

HEART STORY

www.gabrieliqbal.com

www.gabrieliqbal.com

HEART STORY

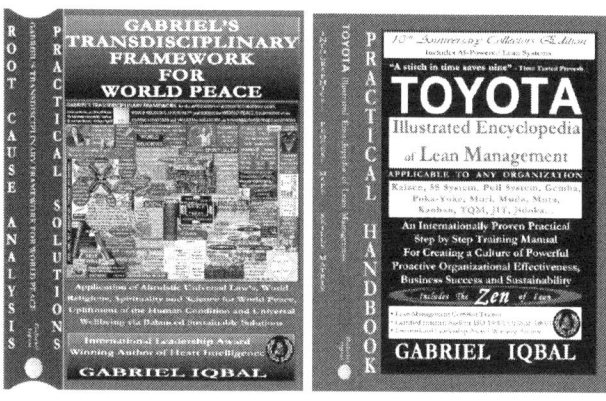

www.eurekamakingadifference.com/illustrated-encyclopedia
www.heartintelligencebook.com
www.gabrieliqbal.com

Coming Soon

www.gabrieliqbal.com

See Everything

*"You are
what you are looking for
in fragmented mirrors
Stop looking
Be Still
End the mind-noise
Silence Now
Eyes shut
Heart wide-open
And then you
See Everything!"*

Gabriel Iqbal

Manufactured by Amazon.ca
Bolton, ON

53518110R00120